PENNY'S JOURNAL
Fortune Lost

A Novella Set in the Forlorn Series

GINA DETWILER

Vinspire Publishing, LLC
www.VinspirePublishing.com

For Cheri
A real-life Penny

I looked on as he opened the sixth seal,
and there was a great earthquake.
The sun became black as funeral clothing,
and the entire moon turned red as blood.
The stars of the sky fell to the earth
as a fig tree drops its fruit
when shaken by a strong wind.
The sky disappeared like a scroll being rolled up,
and every mountain and island was moved from its place.
Then the kings of the earth,
the officials and the generals,
the rich and the powerful,
and everyone, slave and free,
hid themselves in caves and in the rocks of the mountains.
They called to the mountains and the rocks,
"Fall on us and hide us from the face of the one
seated on the throne and from the Lamb's wrath!
The great day of their wrath has come,
and who is able to stand?"
~ Revelation 6:12-17

Author's Note

The events in this book take place during the fifteen years that Jared and Grace were "missing" in the novel *Forbidden*.

YEAR ONE

Gone

May 14

Dear God,

Grace is gone. Again.

Yesterday, I was praising you for bringing her back after she and Jared had disappeared. *That* still seems like a bad dream. An EMP—electromagnetic pulse—hit downtown Buffalo, knocking out the whole power grid in a three-mile radius. There were all kinds of chaos, looting, and stories of a monster out of nightmares tearing up the streets like Godzilla. Jared and Grace went to investigate—they never came home.

But yesterday, I talked to her on the phone. She told a bizarre story of being kidnapped and flown to a castle in Switzerland by that lunatic Darwin Speer. But she and Jared had escaped, and now they were coming home. They just had to get new passports and wait for the airports to re-open after the explosion at CERN shut down half the country, but otherwise, they were fine. Everything was going to be okay.

And now they're gone again. They never went to Bern to get their passports. They never bought plane tickets. It's like they vanished into thin air. I called Grace's phone a hundred times until it started going straight to voicemail. Ripley searched for her phone with GPS but could never pinpoint her exact location.

We're holed up in a motel in Lackawanna because the EMP fried our generator. Ripley, Ralph, Miss Em, and me, along with many other "refugees" from the city. Ripley, our resident hacker, had to buy an old PC from a second-hand store—every place was sold out—and he's searching hospitals and police stations in Switzerland to find Grace and Jared. The Swiss police and the US Embassy aren't too interested in helping—they claim there's no record of Jared and Grace being in the country. Apparently, even if you are kidnapped, you still have to go through customs.

Ripley did manage to track down the couple who helped Grace and Jared after they escaped from Speer. The wife said they had left in a van with their sister-in-law, Josephine, headed to Bern. There were a lot of sinkholes and aftershocks and strange seismic events following the explosion, so they think something happened to them on the road. But their search has come up empty.

Grace Fortune, Jared Lorn—where are you? Lord, can't You tell us?

I don't know how to tell Grace's dad. Silas is still in the hospital, dying of lung cancer. He doesn't have much time left, the doctors say. I was sure Grace would make it home to see him, but now…this will crush him.

At least he got to talk to her yesterday. He didn't tell her how bad it was. Didn't want her to worry. Typical Silas. He's survived so much. He survived Shannon Snow, survived Lester Crow. Are You going to let cancer get him?

I know I should have more faith. Silas does. He's not afraid. He's ready to go home to be with You. But I want him to stay here until Grace comes home. I know I should be praying for Your will, not mine, but I can't help it sometimes.

Ripley says Speer used the EMP to kidnap Jared. Sounds nuts to me, but he's sure of it. Speer stole Jared's DNA to create a "treatment" that cured his fatal disease, and he was planning to sell the treatment to other people. Speer claimed it would not only cure you, but it would make you practically immortal. Like Jared. It also might turn you into a psychopathic maniac. Speer didn't seem concerned about that part.

He's dead, they say. Speer. Died in his bunker when CERN blew up. At first, some people said he survived and was fine, then they said no, they were mistaken. That seemed a little strange. Why did they suddenly change their stories?

I feel bad for Ralph. He's so…sad. Lost. He's been Jared's protector, his guardian angel, for almost all his life. I think he feels as though he's failed somehow.

I have to go to class now. It's hard to focus on studying with all this going on, but at least it gives me something to do, a distraction. I'll visit Silas after. They had to move him to a different hospital after the EMP—it's been a mess.

Maybe I should wait a while before telling him his daughter and son-in-law are missing again. They might still turn up. No need to worry him, right? He's got enough on his mind. Better to let him hope.

I keep thinking of the man with the possessed child who said to You, "I believe; help me with my unbelief!" I get that guy, wanting to trust you, but still not understanding.

My psalm for the day. This was one of Grace's favorites because it was all about singing and making music. For her, music was a weapon against the darkness, against fear, against despair, against evil. That's why I read it today, but this part spoke to me the most.

We put our hope in the Lord.
He is our help and our shield.
In him our hearts rejoice,
for we trust in his holy name.
Let your unfailing love surround us,
Lord, for our hope is in you alone.
~ Psalms 33:20-22

June 9

Dear God,

Back in the Hobbit Hole, finally. It's good to be home after a month in a motel, but it's so empty without Grace and Jared. I miss Jared's guitar, Grace's silly laughter.

Ripley's gone into the Lair—he won't come out unless he smells food. Miss Em stays in the kitchen, mostly. She bakes when she's anxious. At least the smells are better than the motel, which always smelled like stale cigarettes.

Ralph sits in his chair with a book in his lap, not reading. I try to talk to him, ask him questions about stuff he used to love to talk about, but he barely hears me. I'm no substitute for Grace or Jared, I guess.

Still no clue what happened to them. Praying for answers.

Listen to my prayer, LORD!
Because of your faithfulness, hear my requests for mercy!
Because of your righteousness, answer me!
~ Psalms 143:1

June 11

Dear God,

Today I got a call from Grace's number—my heart skipped several beats. But it wasn't her. Instead, a man said he was a police officer from Switzerland. They'd found Grace's phone in a van on the CERN campus and called the last number she had dialed. My number.

I was confused. CERN? Surely, he meant Bern. That's where Grace and Jared had been heading. But no, the officer said the van was at CERN—that place with the giant collider.

I put Ralph on the phone. Suddenly, he sat up straight, his eyes were wide open as he listened, his book dropping to the floor. He asked a lot of questions but didn't seem to get very satisfactory answers. The police said they found the van in a wooded area, but there were no people—or bodies—around. There was a huge hole in the side of the van, perhaps the result of a bomb. But if it had been a bomb, where were the bodies? There was no charring, either, like one would expect from a car bomb. Nothing burned. The police were stumped as to what had caused the hole.

After he hung up, Ralph talked over the situation with Ripley. Maybe it was the monster, Ripley said. The Nephilim monster who had escaped the castle with Jared and Grace. I'd forgotten all about him. Was the monster in the van too? Why hadn't Jared told us about it?

Or maybe it was Jared who did it, I said. Jared was a Nephilim himself, if not a fully formed one. Maybe he had changed. Maybe he knew Speer was in trouble and went to rescue him. Or worse, Jared had decided to join Speer, after all. But what had he done with Grace? And Josephine?

Ralph got up and went to his room, shutting the door behind him. I couldn't blame him. I didn't want to believe it either.

I need a word for today. Help me to believe.

whenever I'm afraid, I put my trust in you—
in God, whose word I praise.
I trust in God; I won't be afraid.
What can mere flesh do to me?
~ Psalms 56:3-4

June 12

Dear God,

Before class today, I went to visit Silas. He looked so much weaker and paler. He had an oxygen tube in his nose and breathed with difficulty. I was prepared to tell him the truth about Grace. I've been telling him that the airports haven't reopened yet, which was the reason for the delay. But I couldn't put it off any longer.

I didn't have to say a word. He was too weak to talk, but he handed me a letter. The envelope said, "For Grace." He smiled and nodded, and in his eyes, I saw he knew the truth and that he forgave me for lying to him. I shoved the letter into my backpack, holding back the tears that threatened.

I heard a soft knock behind me and turned to see someone standing in the doorway, holding a bunch of flowers. My mouth dropped open. It was Mace—Mason.

Let's just say we have a history. Like, he tried to kill me back when he was a drug-addicted Satanist. But then he changed, found Jesus, and got rid of his demons, thanks to Ralph, and maybe me too. I helped with his deliverance. He used to work with Silas in the bike shop, but I hadn't seen him since Grace's wedding. I hadn't been able to reach him—I thought he had just ghosted me.

His hair was combed neatly, and he was growing a beard which made him look so much older. He still had a nose ring, but most of his other piercings were gone. Mason? I said. I tried to hide how glad I was to see him.

He came over and did that bro-arm-clenching thing with Silas and said a few words about how much he appreciated Silas helping him recover and giving him an interest in fixing things. He had enrolled in auto mechanic school. I could see tears in Silas' eyes. He was a former drug addict himself, so I think it made him happy to know he'd changed a life.

When Silas drifted off to sleep, I walked Mason out of the hospital. I told him I missed him, but I was proud of him going to mechanic school. He seemed really happy about that and a little embarrassed. He asked if I'd like to go for a cup of coffee with him. I said I had class, but then I invited him to the Hobbit Hole for dinner. It was kind of an impulse, but I knew Miss Em wouldn't mind, and we all needed a distraction. I told him about

Grace and Jared being missing—he was shocked.

I admit I had a hard time focusing during my class because I was thinking about Mason. It's funny how you can forget the bad stuff about a person once they've changed. But even I was amazed at how much I had forgiven. Here I was, inviting a guy who tried to murder me over for dinner. Isn't that kind of crazy?

I walk all around your altar, LORD,
proclaiming out loud my thanks,
declaring all your wonderful deeds!
~ Psalms 26:6-7

June 14

Dear God,

Dinner with Mason was pretty fun. I was afraid it would be awkward, but Miss Em greeted him with one of her rib-cracking hugs and told him she'd made meatloaf because she remembered how much he loved her meatloaf. Ralph shook Mason's hand and said he was glad to see him. Even Ripley came out of his lair wearing a clean T-shirt.

Mason talked all through dinner, telling us how he much he loved fixing cars, just like he used to love fixing bikes. His program will take a year to complete, but he already had a job working at an auto shop on Prospect. He told us a funny story about this lady who brought in her car saying it had a foul-smelling odor. It really did smell bad—stunk up the whole shop. The main mechanic couldn't figure out what was causing the smell—there didn't seem to be anything wrong with the car. So, Mason started poking around the interior and found a pound of hamburger, expired three months and covered in maggots, under the rear seat. The lady was so mad she had to pay for the service, she called her insurance agent to see if it was covered. Mason could hear the agent laughing on the other end.

Mason also peppered Ralph with questions about things in the Bible he didn't understand. Like why did God curse the ground when Adam and Eve sinned? And why did God prefer Abel's offering to Cain's? And why did God send a worldwide flood and kill all the animals along with the people?

Ralph came back to himself as he talked to Mason, and for a while, things seemed to be almost normal. But as Miss Em served dessert—apple pie with ice cream—the subject turned to Grace and Jared. The light dimmed in Ralph's eyes.

Are you going over there? To Switzerland? Mason asked.

Ralph and I looked at each other. It was a question we'd never asked ourselves before, the most obvious question.

I said maybe we should. Ralph said he would think about it.

Before he left, Mason asked if he could see me again. I said sure. We're going out again tomorrow.

Thank You, Lord. For…everything.

Bless the Lord, O my soul,
and forget not all his benefits,
who forgives all your iniquity,
who heals all your diseases,
who redeems your life from the pit,
who crowns you with steadfast love and mercy,
who satisfies you with good so
that your youth is renewed like the eagle's.
~ Psalms 103: 1-5

June 23

Dear God,

Silas is with You now.

It's still hard to write that—to admit it's true. I was there with him—the nurse called me at the library to say I should come. Ralph, Miss Em, and Mason came too. We sang "Amazing Grace" as he took his last breaths. I swear I saw angels surrounding his bed, singing with us.

My heart breaks for Grace. Maybe she's already there, with You, waiting to greet him. Some part of me still believes she's alive. Somewhere.

We had a memorial service at Silo City, where he was living when Grace found him. Mason tracked down some members of the Silo City Collective, a band that used to play together there on summer nights, to sing some of his favorite songs. Mason talked about how Silas showed him how to fix bikes and how much better it felt to fix things than to break them. A guy named Jim, a guitar player with the Collective, talked about the time Silas coaxed Jared to play guitar with them. I told of how Silas had protected Jared when Lester Crow made him join his demonic rock band, Blood Moon. Ralph gave a short sermon about how the biblical Silas had looked after and protected Paul just as Silas had protected Grace and Jared through the years. By the end, everyone was in tears, even Mason. Everyone except for me.

For some reason, I just couldn't cry.

When the speeches were over, we drank punch, and Miss Em passed out cookies. We tossed Silas' ashes over the Buffalo River, right outside the silos.

First Grace and Jared. Now Silas. Lord, I know you have everything under control, but…my heart hurts so bad. Help me understand.

When we got home, I went to my room, shut the door, and pulled Silas' letter out of my backpack. I thought maybe I should read it. Why not? They're both gone. But I didn't. It's not for me. Besides, I still had hope that Grace would come back. I would save it for her.

Then the door opened. I was about to yell at whoever had just barged into my room, but it was Mason. He asked if I was okay. I was kind of short with him and told him I was fine. Silas wasn't my dad, after all. I told him he should go home.

He didn't leave. He asked me about my real father. I said I had never met him. And then I told him the whole story. I did try and meet my father, once. My mother had told me his name. I went to his house. A woman came to the door, and I told her who I was. She called out for my father to come to the door and meet me, but he refused. She shrugged and said she was sorry and closed the door in my face.

I thought You were like that, once. A father who didn't want to know me, who turned his back when I was born, and pretended I didn't exist. I think a lot of people get their own fathers and You mixed up.

Mason told me his dad had left when he was a kid. Mason had put a hex on him, and he'd died of a heart attack. For years, Mason took credit for killing his father. When he first realized Jesus was real, he was so overcome with guilt—not just for thinking he'd killed his own dad, but for what he did to me and lots of other people—he wanted to kill himself. He couldn't believe Jesus would forgive him. Silas had shown him that Jesus really did forgive. And heal.

That did it. The tears came pouring out of me. I sobbed so hard my stomach cramped. I bent over and felt Mason sit next to me, his hand on my back, telling me it was going to be all right.

He will wipe away every tear from their eyes,
And death shall be no more,
neither shall there be mourning, nor crying,
nor pain anymore,
for the former things have passed away.
~ Rev 21:4

July 1

Dear God,

We're in Switzerland, Ralph and me, at a little Gasthaus in Ste-Genis-Pouilly, the town where Jared was born. In 1859. So weird to think that.

Yesterday, we went to Schoenberg to meet the couple—Karl and Greta—who took in Grace and Jared after they escaped from the castle. Greta told us how our friends had come upon the home of her sister-in-law, Josephine, who lived over the mountain. They claimed to be lost American hikers. Josephine had driven them to Karl's gas station so they could use the phone and internet. They had left the next day in Josephine's van. Josephine was also missing, and they were worried. Now that her van had turned up in CERN, they feared the worst.

Greta told us that Josephine was "a little crazy" and had a lot of imaginary friends, but she would never do anything to harm others. When Ralph asked if anyone else had been with them, Greta translated for Karl, who shook his head. But he didn't look at us. I had a strong feeling he was hiding something, but he never spoke a word.

We drove to CERN this morning in a little rented Citroen. Roadblocks prevented us from getting onto the campus. It took an hour of negotiating with the police to get us an escort to see the van once Ralph explained who we were. They said we could only stay for an hour due to possible radiation exposure.

Three Swiss officers accompanied us to the site. The van was half-hidden by trees in a remote area—no wonder it had gone unnoticed for so long. There wasn't much inside—blankets, a bag of food, and a large cape with a hood made of fabric scraps. Ralph and I exchanged looks. Big enough to fit a Nephilim? I asked him. His eyes got wide, then they closed altogether. His shoulders shook like he was crying, but he didn't make any sound. Was it the Nephilim? Or was it Jared?

We searched the woods but found no evidence of human or animal or monster remains. That was almost a relief. But as we came out of the woods, I noticed orange fencing covered by plastic tarps in the distance. What's that? I asked the officer. The crater, he said. The site of the explosion. The police had thoroughly investigated it—there were no bodies in there.

But I could feel them.

I can't explain it. You gave me a gift. Discerning spirits, Paul called it. It's not something I asked for. Maybe because demons have hounded me for so much of my life—I know when they are present. My vision goes all gray and fuzzy, and my skin gets cold. And there's a weight on my chest, like something pressing, making it hard to breathe.

Something was there. In that hole. A darkness like nothing I'd felt before.

My whole body shook like it might break apart. My legs went out from under me. I must have fainted. The next thing I knew, the officer was kneeling over me, his brows knit together. He helped me up and asked me if I needed water. I told him I was fine, took Ralph's arm, and led him back to the car.

On the way to the Gasthaus, I told Ralph what I thought. There was something in that hole, an evil spirit perhaps. Could our friends have fallen in, never to be discovered? Or was it something else?

I opened my Bible and read this.

I would have despaired unless I had believed
that I would see the goodness of the Lord
In the land of the living.
Wait for the Lord;
Be strong and let your heart take courage;
Yes, wait for the Lord.
~ Psalms 27: 13-14

July 3

Dear God,

The police said they would conduct forensic tests on the cloak found in the van, as well as the van itself, something they had so far neglected to do. When we get home, we'll have to send some items—hairbrushes, toothbrushes, anything with Jared's and Grace's DNA. It's going to be a long time before we get answers. Not that we are expecting any.

Last night, Ralph and I ate dinner in a small cafe in Geneva, and he told me about the early days when he was a boy, and Jared was his "big brother." He told me stories I had never heard before about Jared's travels into the Canadian West, when he got mixed up with some doomsday cult, and Ralph went out to rescue him.

I was always there to rescue him, Ralph said. No matter what sort of trouble he got himself into, I could always get him out of it.

I knew what he was thinking—he had failed this time. Why didn't Jared confide in him? Why didn't Jared tell him he was going to CERN? With a Nephilim monster?

I reached across the table and took his hand.

We'll get through this, I said. It sounded lame, but it was all I could think of. And then I told him that I thought they were still alive. Otherwise, we would have found some trace of them. They'll come home. I was sure of it.

He looked hopeful then. He almost smiled.
They'll come home.
Won't they?
But now, Lord, what do I look for?

My hope is in you.
Hear my prayer, Lord, listen to my cry for help;
do not be deaf to my weeping.
~ Psalms 39:7,12

YEAR FIVE

Virus

May 12

Dear God,

I graduated from college today.

Ralph, Miss Em, and Ripley came to the ceremony at the university auditorium. Mason came too. He stood up and whistled when they called my name. I was so embarrassed.

Afterward, we went out for dinner at an Irish pub. We didn't talk about how Jared and Grace have now been missing for five years, almost to the day. We'd stopped talking about it long ago, even though it was still on our minds, especially in May. It's not that we've stopped looking. It's just that we've run out of places to look.

I haven't given up yet, but it gets harder every year. Whenever I ask You for an answer, You always give me the same story: the disciples locked in the upper room the day after Jesus' death, thinking he was gone forever. And being so wrong.

But how long before they come back?

Miss Em asked me what I planned to do now that I was a college graduate. I told her I wanted to go to seminary. Maybe get a Master's in Divinity.

They all stopped talking when I said that. They know how hard school was for me, with my brain issues, and trying to earn my way because I didn't want to take money from Ralph. Working at Turning Pages bookshop didn't pay all that well, but I loved the job because I could read any book in the store when things were slow. And they also let me order books I wanted—books about You. They never had much of a religion section, this being Buffalo and all, but I stocked the shelves with C. S. Lewis, Philip Yancy, and other favorites. I wanted to learn as much as I could, so I had the right words when people asked about You. It's the one thing we believers still aren't very good at.

Ralph said divinity school was a fine idea, and he would be glad to help with the tuition. Miss Em patted my hand and told me I was very wise. That made me blush.

As we were leaving, I looked up to see Harry Ravel come on the TV over the bar. I stopped in my tracks and stared at the screen. The words under Harry's face read, "Harry Ravel, Governor of California, running for President of the United States." He was talking, showing off his shiny smile, and right next to him with an equally shiny smile plastered on her face stood Shannon Snow. His wife.

Grace's mother.

I was really glad for once that Grace wasn't around to see this.

Lord, he can't win, can he? You can't let that man be president. No way.

Ripley said he has a good chance of winning, cause he's super popular in California and he's got nice hair, and he's good-looking, and his wife is beautiful. People love that stuff. These days, that's all that matters, I guess. Not what's on the inside, only what's on the outside.

Then the video on the TV switched to images of people lying in hospital beds with red rashes all over their bodies. The words running across the bottom of the screen said, "New Ebola-like virus ravaging the Middle East." I'd never heard a thing about it.

Ripley said it had started in Israel and was spreading into Europe, Asia, and Africa. There were a few cases in America, too. The symptoms were similar to a milder form of Ebola—high fever, headache, abdominal pain, and painful rashes. But unlike Ebola, this virus seemed to be transmitted through the air, which made it much more contagious. It was so new that the medical experts didn't even have a name for it.

As I watched the images of sick people flash by on the screen, some of them with blood leaking from their eyes, I prayed this psalm over and over:

> *The LORD will strengthen them*
> *when they are lying in bed, sick.*
> *You will completely transform the place where they lie ill.*
> *~ Psalms 41:3*

May 25

Dear God,

Something amazing happened today—I know You already

know this, but I'm going to tell You anyway because I almost don't believe it myself.

Mason came into the bookstore and asked if I could take a walk. I said I was working—couldn't he see that? —and maybe I could meet him later. He seemed really anxious about something, and he asked if I could just take a break for ten minutes. I finally asked my boss, and she said fine in a huffy voice.

I admit I was a little annoyed too. My boss is already a cranky person, and I didn't need her madder at me. Besides, I hadn't even heard from Mason for two weeks. Why was he suddenly all bothered about talking to me?

So, I walked outside with him, and it was raining, of course, and I was getting even more irritated because I didn't have an umbrella or a coat. And he wasn't even saying anything important, just asking how things were going, stuff like that, and I was like, I really need to get back to work. I turned around and headed back to the store. Then suddenly, he grabbed my arm and spun me around and got down on one knee and asked me to marry him.

Just. Like. That.

I was like, what did you say? I thought I was dreaming or something. But there he was, on his knees, and people on the sidewalk stopped to look and snicker, and some of them whipped out phones. He dug around in his pockets and came up with a ring—a tiny little diamond on a silver band—and presented it to me like it was the most precious thing in the world. I just stared at his face, rain dripping off his hair into his eyes, so he had to blink constantly. And I burst out laughing.

Yes, I did.

Not that I thought it was a joke. I was just so…shocked. Everything I did was completely inappropriate.

He got this look on his face like I'd smacked him. Puzzled. Deflated.

But then I said yes.

I held out my hand so he could slip the ring on my finger. Perfect fit. I didn't care about the rain anymore.

He got up and kissed me—I think it was the first time he'd really kissed me like a boy is supposed to kiss a girl, at least in my dreams.

Then he told me he'd loved me for a long time, but he was

always afraid to tell me so because he'd hurt me so badly in the past, and he didn't know if that made it so I couldn't love him. Because he wasn't worthy of love or something. I told him that was nonsense, and I told him of course I loved him, and what took him so long anyway? He apologized for that, and I said to stop apologizing already, and I kissed him again to shut him up. It worked.

> *Who is as great a god as you, God?*
> *You are the God who works wonders.*
> *~ Psalms 77: 13-14*

September 1

Dear God,

We postponed the wedding again. This virus is really getting on my nerves.

Why Lord? We were just starting to move on after Grace and Jared, after Silas. I was going to marry Mason and start a new chapter of life when this happens? The city's been in lockdown all summer. Churches closed, restaurants closed, schools didn't reopen this fall. Mason is on furlough from his job with no pay. Ralph invited him to stay at the Hobbit Hole in Jared's old room. At least I get to see him more often.

We wanted a real wedding in a church. We go to this little church on Grant called "Jesus Saves." I'm not sure if that's the name of the church or just the slogan. Blaine Humphries is the pastor, a young guy from the streets, a former drug addict just like us. He said he would marry us back in June. But then the lockdowns happened, and all the businesses, including churches, had to close. We postponed until September, but the lockdowns have been extended indefinitely now.

Buffalo is a ghost town. The only cars on the road are delivery drivers for Door Dash and Amazon, it seems. It's worse than after the EMP. Even football was canceled.

They say this virus is really bad. Hospitals are overrun. People report that the itching makes them want to die. Then the rashes turn into blisters and ooze—sounds gross. It's worse among older people and those who are already sick with something else. Every day the death toll flashes on the TV screen, going up and up.

Experts on TV say we all have to stay home until the virus is brought under control and we have a vaccine. How long will that be? They also say the virus came from a lab in Israel. Now everyone is mad at Israel. People on social media are calling for Israel to pay. Things are getting crazy.

Ripley said it's pretty fishy that this virus came along when it did, considering that the Interlaken Group had hosted the Tomorrow Agenda just a few months before. The Tomorrow Agenda was this big summit meeting where a bunch of scientific and political elites wargamed how to deal with a worldwide pandemic. He's making a video about the meeting for his YouTube channel, which is called YBR—it stands for Yellow Brick Road. It's where he and his online buddies post all their conspiracy theories.

Prayer for today: Make a way for Mason and me to get married. End this terrible disease, please! Help me understand why this is happening. This psalm says it better than I could.

The LORD is close to everyone
who calls out to him,
to all who call out to him sincerely.
God shows favor to those who honor him,
listening to their cries for help and saving them.
~ Psalms 145:18-19

September 15

Dear God,

I'm an official felon now.

It all started so innocently. I got an email from Pastor Blaine. He was holding a prayer meeting in Delaware Park. We can't meet inside, he said, so we'll meet outside. I was excited, so Mason and I went.

There were about a dozen people there with Blaine, and a guy named Joe playing the guitar. He reminded me a little of Jared. He sang *Amazing Grace*. Of course. That song just gets to me, makes me think of Grace. I don't want to be reminded of that.

Blaine read some scripture and gave a little sermon about endurance, and then we prayed for people suffering due to the lockdowns and the virus—everyone had been touched in some way. It felt so good to be among believers again. To just cry out to You.

Until the cops showed up.

They weren't actually cops. They were HASOs—Health and Safety Officers, dispatched by the state to ensure people complied with the lockdown rules. Two guys on bicycles, masks obscuring their faces. They interrupted the singing and wanted to see Blaine's permit for the gathering. He said he didn't know he needed a permit—that was some new rule apparently. They told us we couldn't sing because it was a "super spreader" activity. Another new rule.

I started recording everything with my phone. The HASO yelled at me to put the phone down. I said I had a right to record anything that happened in public. He asked me where my mask was. I said I didn't need one since I was outside. He shouted that I was supposed to wear a mask, even outdoors—he was so angry he fogged up his face shield. Sorry, Lord, but I smart-mouthed that guy. I asked him to show me where that law was written. That just made him madder.

Mason tried to intervene, but he shoved Mason so hard he fell. That was it—I got fired up. I started yelling at the man to stop harassing us, and soon, everyone was yelling. The other HASO radioed the police. Almost immediately, several cop cars showed up. They charged me, Mason, Blaine, and several others with disorderly conduct and violating a local ordinance by meeting without a permit, singing, and failure to follow masking protocols. They took us to the police station. I called Ripley to tell him—he laughed out loud but said he would come to bail us out.

I sat in a cell with a woman named Mabel, who was really high on crack and wouldn't stop swearing at me, calling me all kinds of names. I told Mabel You loved her. She said some bad words in response to that. I figured it couldn't hurt, so I told her my story, and how I would be just like her if You hadn't saved me, and that pretty much everyone I knew from my time on the streets was dead or in jail. When Mabel asked me why I was there, I told her about the prayer meeting. She smirked and asked me why Jesus let me get arrested. I told her maybe it was so I could meet her and talk to her about You. She rolled her eyes and laughed.

When the guard came to let me out, I asked for a pen and wrote my number on Mabel's hand in case she ever wanted to talk things over. She didn't say anything, but she kept staring at her hand.

When we got back to the Hobbit Hole, I showed Ripley, Ralph, and Miss Em the video I'd made of the HASOs. Ripley asked if he could post it on YBR. Mason said it felt like we were living in the land of Oz these days.

Ripley added some cool music and effects to my video and had Miss Em do a voice-over because she has this sweet but also sassy "Auntie Em" voice. Within a few days, the video had thousands of views.

People began sending Ripley their own videos, some of which were shocking. A woman in a car was arrested for being twenty miles from her home without an "essential" purpose. A hair salon owner was fined ten thousand dollars and spent a week in jail for doing someone's hair against lockdown orders. A family home was raided because neighbors had reported more than ten people had gathered there for a birthday party. The home owner spent a night in jail and had to pay a five thousand dollar fine.

At the same time, fear of the virus spreading in prison populations led to the early release of many criminals, even convicted murderers. Then the governor of New York passed a law suspending bail requirements, so offenders were simply let go.

I need a word from You about all this. Because I am just so confused right now. What's going on? Ralph says it's only the beginning. Beginning of what? I'm praying for everyone to come to their senses again. Have mercy on us, Lord, because we don't know what we're doing.

Don't remember the iniquities of past generations;
let your compassion hurry to meet us because we've been brought so
low.
~ *Psalms 79:8*

November 5

Dear God,

Harry Ravel is now President of the United States.

He campaigned on his plan to end the virus, although he didn't actually say what that plan was. Not that anyone cared—people are so desperate to do something about the virus they will take any promise they can get. And Harry has always been good at making people believe him.

So now Shannon Snow is First Lady of the USA.

What would Grace say?

Ravel also promised to make Israel pay for creating the virus. Some of the Arab countries claim Israeli scientists were secretly working on a bioweapon that would affect only people of Arab descent. Israel denied it. But Turkey has already declared war on Israel, and Syria, Iran, Iraq, the UAE, and Saudi Arabia are joining in. The presidents of Russia and China have pledged support. This could be the start of World War Three.

Ripley still thinks the Interlaken Group is behind the whole thing. William West has got Speer's Nephilim Makeover treatment, he says, and he's itching to use it. What better way than to manufacture a virus? Ripley says Ravel will soon announce that they have already come up with a vaccine, and it will be ready for distribution in a matter of weeks.

I can't believe that. Speer's treatment is too dangerous. Even William West wouldn't go that far.

Ripley said I was being naïve. It's all part of West's game plan to take over every facet of human life. He's considered the greatest philanthropist in the world, even winning the Nobel prize for developing GMO-farming techniques that were supposed to save Africa from starvation. Ripley's made a ton of videos about West and his company, AgroSolutions. His "solutions" have only made the food problem in Africa worse, but the media keeps singing his praises as some great savior. He must have a great PR department.

We still meet for prayer in the park, in a woodsy area where the HASOs don't usually bother us, especially now that it's getting cold. There have been new people coming, too—word is getting around. Even in this dark time, some lights continue to shine.

Because your steadfast love is better than life,
my lips will praise you.
So I will bless you as long as I live;
in your name I will lift up my hands.
~ Psalms 63:3-4

YBR Podcast #14

Friends, Auntie Em here. We are definitely not in Kansas any-more. You have all seen the Instagram photos of the quarantine camps for those who either test positive or come in contact with an infected person. They have bulldozed much of the real estate on the east side and put up long, steel buildings they call "cabins," though they claim the measure is only temporary and the cabins are very nice inside, on par with a luxury hotel. It's like going on vacation, they say.

The government is so determined to make the camps appeal-ing that it pays influencers to promote them on their accounts. See this picture of a girl standing on a porch, smiling as she takes a selfie? Well, our own ultra-sneaky Lollypop Guild has gotten a hold of some actual photos. Do you see those chain-link fences? Armed guards? Do those buildings look like cozy cabins? Does anything about these camps look like a vacation?

We received a video from a woman who recently got out of a camp. Here's her story.

[Video of young woman, looking wan and distraught]

"I got a call from someone asking if I had been with so and so on a certain day, and I said no. I lied. Within an hour, a blue van with the HASO logo pulled up in front of my building, along with two police cars. Two HASOs and three cops came to my door and told me to pack a bag. They knew I had lied, and I had to go with them. My roommate recorded the whole thing. [show re-cording of the arrest]

"They took me to this building that was set up like a clinic. First, they gave me a test. I tested negative. But it didn't matter. I still had to stay at the camp for a week. I didn't protest—I was too scared. They brought me to this room—it was more like a cell in a prison than a hotel. Every day they came in wearing their

Hazmat suits to test me and drop off food in a paper bag. The food was awful. Other than that, I didn't see anyone. They had taken my phone, so I couldn't take pictures or call anyone. By the way, there are no porches on these buildings. There was a TV in the room, so I watched TV all day because there was nothing else to do. The only stations I got were news shows about how terrible the virus was, even though I didn't know anyone who had gotten sick. When I complained that I needed to get some exercise, they sent someone to walk me up and down the street for ten minutes.

"They finally let me go after I'd tested negative for seven straight days. One of the people there told me that if I hadn't lied in the first place, I would only have been in for three days. I guess the message was, tell your friends not to lie when we call. Oh, and today I got a bill for three thousand dollars for my 'hotel accommodations.'" (She laughs, though there are tears in her eyes) "I got fired from my job because I didn't show up, and now I have this huge bill I can't pay. I don't know what to do." [End of video]

I wish I could say this story was unusual. But many of you have shared similar stories with us, which we will highlight in the coming days. We've already received warnings from YouTube that the content of these videos is "misleading," but we are here to share the truth, no matter how uncomfortable. Jesus told us that the truth shall set us free. Sadly, though, most people don't want to hear it. They believe what they want to believe and choose their facts accordingly.

Here's another uncomfortable fact. Sick people are not getting treated. They are told to quarantine at home and not go to a clinic or hospital unless their condition becomes severe. We have seen doctors on the Internet speaking out against this policy and testifying that they have used readily available medicines to mitigate the disease. Their videos have been removed, and the drugs they promote have mysteriously disappeared from pharmacies. That seems to us a strange turn of events. Check the link in the comments section if you want to reach any of these doctors directly.

Remember, the way they will control you is through fear. But God did not give you a spirit of fear, Paul told Timothy, but a spirit of Power and Love and Self-control. Power to overcome trials of this world in his Name, love to care for others and work together, and self-control to act wisely, to seek after truth, to not be ruled by emotions. The enemy does not want you to access the power of the Holy Spirit—he wants you to cower in fear. Be bold and courageous! He that is in you is greater than he that is in the world. Please share this video with your friends. God bless you.

December 3

Dear God,

Blaine organized a prayer vigil on the steps of City Hall tonight. Ripley announced it on YBR. We are gathering to pray for our city, for the sick, for those who have lost their jobs because of the lockdowns, and for those who have taken to drugs and alcohol out of despair. Blaine put together a whole worship band, and he will preach the gospel to whoever comes. The city gave him a permit—he thinks that's a hopeful sign that things might be changing.

I hope he's right. Please watch over us tonight, Lord. Bring your people together to pray. And protect us from evil.

Because…I have this weird feeling. The dark is lurking just around the corner.

Because you have made the Lord your dwelling place—
the Most High, who is my refuge —
no evil shall be allowed to befall you,
no plague come near your tent.
~ Psalms 91:9-10

YEAR SIX

Cure

January 4

Dear God,

First night home after a month in jail.

Did I do the right thing?

Wish I had my journal in jail. I could have talked to You more about it. I talk better when I'm writing things down. When I just think things, the thoughts get all jumbled in my head. Part of my brain problem, I guess.

The prayer vigil started so well. More than a thousand people came! I couldn't believe the turnout. We handed out candles—the whole of Niagara Square was lit up. People were singing hymns and Christmas carols, lifting their voices in praise. Blaine had to use a megaphone, but he spoke with power and truth. And we prayed—boy, did we pray! The band played, and we sang until our throats were dry, and we chanted and praised, and we got real, real loud.

For a while, I forgot about my misgivings. It was all so beautiful. Our worship chased away all the unclean spirits—or so I thought.

It started with smoke—black smoke filling the square. A car was on fire. Then more cars. Then an explosion. Like a bomb. People started screaming and running in all directions, trampling each other. Blaine shouted for order, trying to get people to calm down, and then some people dressed all in black jumped up on the platform, grabbed the megaphone, and began chanting "Freedom!" and "God Rules!" while they thrust their fists into the air. They wore masks so no one knew who they were.

There were sirens and cops everywhere. Mason and I tried to run, but we got blasted by a water cannon—it knocked us back ten feet at least. We ended up on the ground, getting trampled. I groped for Mason's arm, something to hold on to. I couldn't see anything. Someone grabbed my shoulder, turned me over on my stomach, and wrenched my arms behind my back. I felt the cold clasp of handcuffs.

Next thing I knew, I was in a police van. Mason wasn't with me anymore. There were others in the van, too—some girls were crying. They herded us into a jail cell, where we spent the night.

We prayed together—I reminded them of Paul and Silas in prison, and we sang. But the jail doors didn't burst open.

They held us for thirty days in prison until the trial, where we got convicted of civil disobedience, time served. I found Mason after my release—he'd gotten the same sentence. About sixty of us altogether. Mason told me one of the worshippers had been killed. A young woman. A cop thought she was armed and shot her—she'd been holding a cross. The cop was exonerated.

Blaine got six months for instigating the riot, even though plenty of witnesses said the real instigators were Stoners, a drug gang famous for disrupting religious assemblies. The judge didn't care.

Ravel took full advantage of the situation, making a speech denouncing the religious zealots who had "destroyed an entire city block and countless lives." An exaggeration if there ever was one. In response, the city shut down all religious gatherings. None of the Stoners were ever arrested.

Ralph says we are living in the days of Nero. I didn't really understand that, but Miss Em says it was because Nero blamed the burning of Rome on the Christians so he could kill them with impunity. But Miss Em says that Nero most likely started the fires himself.

Well, it worked.

Lord, why didn't you protect us? Why are you letting them win?

Save me, O God!
For the waters have come up to my neck.
I sink in deep mire,
where there is no foothold;
I have come into deep waters,
and the flood sweeps over me.
I am weary with my crying out;
my throat is parched.
My eyes grow dim
with waiting for my God.
~ Psalms 69: 1-3

YBR Podcast #25

[VIDEO shots of scientists working in labs, testing animals, Len Wilder making speeches, Ravel making speeches, etc.]

Greetings, Munchkins, Auntie Em here. We knew it was coming, didn't we? First the virus, now the Cure! A miracle cure, they are calling it. A super-vaccine, less than nine months after the start of the worst pandemic in a millennium. But this vaccine offers immunity not just to this virus, but to all diseases known to mankind. It means an end to this pandemic and all future pandemics, as well as cancer, genetic diseases, you name it. Humans will once again live for hundreds of years, as they did at the beginning of time.

You might be wondering how they came up with a cure so quickly. We here in Kansas happen to have some inside information. You see, this vaccine is not a vaccine at all, but a new kind of gene therapy created by the late, great Darwin Speer. You might remember how he cured himself of his own fatal genetic disease some years ago? And his plans to share his discovery with the whole world?

We believe this new Cure is a clever rebranding of Speer's miracle treatment. But here's the part you need to understand: Speer made his treatment from Nephilim DNA.

Now, now, I hear you shouting into your computer screens: Auntie Em, have you lost your marbles? Nephilim haven't existed for thousands of years! Well, I could ask you this: how do you know? They existed after the Flood, and they weren't entirely wiped out by the Conquest, were they? Nephilim are half-angel, which means they are practically immortal—they could survive for centuries.

We can't tell you everything about how we know these things, but we can tell you that this Cure has extreme side effects, not the least being death. A trial secretly conducted in Africa—nothing gets past our Lollipop Guild—resulted in a twenty percent death rate, with another forty percent experiencing severe and crippling side effects. Being that it took place in Africa, the media ignored it.

Speeracles now reports a ninety percent success rate in their latest trials, though the details have not been released to the public. The world doesn't seem to want to know the details; it is so desperate for an end to the virus. The Swiss government has already greenlit the Cure, along with several other European countries. The WHO has proclaimed it the only real hope for the world. The CDC and the FDA have moved forward with emergency authorization here in the US.

We must warn you that this Cure might very well be worse than the disease. Do you believe you can trust your government and Speeracles to tell you the truth?

Do your research, Munchkins! Remember the words of Jesus' brother, James, someone well familiar with rooting out the truth:

> *If you need wisdom, ask our generous God, and he will give it to you... Do not waver, for a person with divided loyalty is as unsettled as a wave of the sea that is blown and tossed by the wind. Such people should not expect to receive anything from the Lord. Their loyalty is divided between God and the world, and they are unstable in everything they do.*
> ~ James 1:5-8

February 9

Dear God,

Our Cure video went live yesterday. The response has been overwhelming, but not at all what we bargained for. People are *angry*. At us!

> Why are you being so negative? Obviously, the Cure worked great for Darwin Speer. Why don't you want us to get the same protection he got?
> Why do you guys always have to look on the bad side? This is actually a good thing!
> We need a cure! We want to get back to normal! Stop being Debbie Downers!
> Nephilim DNA? You guys have really gone off the deep end. I'm unsubscribing now.

Thousands unsubscribed. And YouTube zapped us with a strike for false and misleading content.

I don't know what to think. If our subscribers don't believe us, who will? Maybe we shouldn't have mentioned the Nephilim thing. Mason thought it was a bad idea. People weren't ready for that. I was the one who pushed it.

Mason says that whatever happens, we have to keep speaking the truth. That's what Jesus would do.

Did we do the right thing? I memorized this psalm today. I need to remember who's really in charge.

God is our refuge and strength,
a very present help in trouble.
Therefore we will not fear
though the earth gives way,
though the mountains be moved
into the heart of the sea,
though its waters roar and foam,
though the mountains tremble at its swelling.
~ Psalms 46: 1-3

YBR Podcast #29

Well, Munchkins, we have been investigating the allegations that Israel is the source of the virus that is wreaking havoc around the world. Forgive us for being skeptical of the narrative propagated by the Ozzies, but you know us. We're just the suspicious types.

Here's their version: the Israelis created a deadly pathogen that would attack only people with Arab DNA using dangerous and illegal gain-of-function research. One virus strain used in the research escaped from the lab in Tel Aviv, either intentionally or accidentally, infecting the entire world.

But things aren't adding up. How could a virus created to attack only a specific genetic type infect everyone in the world? The Israelis deny conducting such research. They claim the only labs working on creating new viruses are in China and the United States.

The Guild has done its own research. This tale of an Arab-targeted virus was reported by one media outlet over twenty years ago and never confirmed. A scientist we spoke to said the idea itself was absurd—Jews and Arabs are far too genetically similar to make such a virus feasible.

We do know that William West, founder of the Interlaken Group, owns a controlling stake in Speeracles, the company that makes the Cure. Leonard Wilder, Darwin Speer's chief medical consultant, is the president of the company and an advisor to the CDC. West, though a Jew himself, originally from Poland, was the first to denounce Israel for creating the virus. Interestingly, he is also the second largest contributor to the World Health Organization.

What does all this mean? Things are never what they seem. Jesus warned his disciples: "Look, I'm sending you as sheep among wolves. Therefore, be wise as serpents and innocent as doves." Matthew 10:16

Pray for wisdom and discernment. And be prepared for persecution if you resist—it's coming. Remember these words of Jesus—I think they apply today just as they did two thousand years ago.

> *Watch out for people—because they will hand you over to councils and they will beat you in their synagogues. They will haul you in front of governors and even kings because of me so that you may give your testimony to them… Brothers and sisters will hand each other over to be executed. A father will turn his child in. Children will defy their parents and have them executed. Everyone will hate you on account of my name. But whoever stands firm until the end will be saved.*
> ~ *Matthew 10:17-22*

June 7

Dear God,

Tel Aviv is under siege—relentless missile strikes from Syria and Turkey. Thankfully, Israel's Iron Dome is blocking most of them. It looks like some crazy fireworks show. How long can this go on? Videos on social media show people praying in the streets for You to deliver them.

Will You?

They call themselves the Alliance for Justice—almost all the

Muslim countries united to wipe out Israel. Russia, China, Sweden, Germany, and even France are backing them with money and weapons. The UN passed a resolution condemning Israel for creating the virus, even though there is still no actual proof.

Harry—President Ravel—refused to meet with the Israeli prime minister, who has been begging him for help. Ravel says he will follow the lead of the EU and the UN. Congress is even considering sending aid to the Alliance.

No one here seems to care that much about the war. They just want the Cure—they are lining up around the block, even though it's like zero degrees out. The media are full of pictures of people freezing as they wait in line with their QR codes ready. The Cure isn't a shot or a pill but an infusion that takes over an hour.

The weird thing is they aren't offering the Cure to the most vulnerable first, like the elderly and the sick. People have to apply online and meet a bunch of criteria based on age, race, job, economic status, and history of addiction. Ravel says that the underserved and marginalized will be first in line—the homeless, the poor, drug addicts, and criminals.

Ripley said it's all by design. What design? They're building an army, he said. Crazy old Rip. I thought he might be losing it. These lockdowns are making us all a little crazy.

And then yesterday, Mason and I went to a grocery store that was still open to pick up milk and eggs for Miss Em. The place was like a war zone—broken windows, trash all over, and huge guys in hoodies looting the store and beating people up. Victims lay everywhere, moaning and crying. I pulled out my phone to record it all. One looter wasn't wearing a shirt—he had white hair and a tattoo of intertwined snakes on his arm.

Mason called 911. The operator said she already knew of the situation and police were on their way. Where were they? The looters finally ran off, and Mason and I went over to see if we could help the injured people.

One old lady's face was so bloody I thought she was dead until she coughed and groaned. Others had broken arms, big gashes on their heads, bloody noses. Bystanders wandered by, recording on their phones but not stopping to help. Many went in to take more stuff from the store. Mason ran into the store to find bandages.

It was another hour before an ambulance came, and a single

cop car. The ambulance driver told me attacks like this were happening all over the city. There weren't enough ambulances or cops to get to all the scenes.

We went back to the Hobbit Hole with no milk or eggs and told Ralph and Ripley what happened. We watched the video I'd taken, and Ralph asked Ripley to enlarge the tattoo from the white-haired guy's arm. Several snakes wrapped around a spear.

It's the logo for Speeracles, Ripley said.

The white hair, I said. Like Jared. The others had been wearing hoodies, but maybe they all had white hair. Had they had all gotten the Cure?

Ripley is going to post the video tomorrow. We'll see what happens.

Whenever I'm afraid, I put my trust in you—
in God, whose word I praise. I trust in God;
I won't be afraid. What can mere flesh do to me?
~ Psalms 56:3-4

June 10

Dear God,

The response to the video has been—surprising. The first comments were skeptical—we were making a mountain out of a molehill. But then we started getting videos from all over the world with similar stories: white-haired thugs looting stores, beating up random people on the street, stealing cars and crashing them into buildings for no apparent reason, and setting buildings on fire. Nighttime in major city centers has become a hellscape of fires and screaming thugs terrorizing anyone who dares to walk the streets. Ripley posted the videos as fast as he got them, until YouTube shut down his channel for a week's suspension and removed all the videos of the so-called *Ragers*. Ripley knew that was going to happen, so he had already posted on several other sites.

We are in this for real now. No going back. Lord, make us brave.

I bless the Lord who gives me counsel;
in the night also my heart instructs me.

I have set the Lord always before me;
because he is at my right hand,
I shall not be shaken.
~ Psalms 16: 7-8

July 11

Dear God,

We had to cancel the wedding again.

Not because we got cold feet or anything. The church burned down.

Blaine's little church is gone.

Mason and I went to see for ourselves. Ragers had completely shattered the window with "Jesus Saves" painted on it. The whole inside of the building was like a black hole. It still smelled burnt.

Blaine wasn't there, thank You. He lived on the second floor of the building, but he'd been off distributing food to members of his congregation who couldn't leave their homes. He knew it was Ragers that did it because they left their calling card, the snake symbol spray painted on what was left of the inside wall, along with the words "God will burn."

Ever since the riot, this has been happening. Churches vandalized. Pastors arrested if they hold a church service. Not just Buffalo, either. Ravel has directed the Justice Department to investigate church leaders who dare speak out against the government mandates or criticize its handling of the pandemic. Everyone is scared.

Mason took it bad. I told him we could get married anywhere—it didn't have to be in a church. Even though we both wanted a real wedding, with the whole walking down the aisle thing, it wasn't necessary. But he's just mad, really mad. It's like I'm seeing the old Mason—Mace—coming out of him. That makes me scared.

I needed a word from You. For my city. My church. My home. My family. My fiancé. I always go back to Psalm 46.

God is in that city, and so it will not be shaken.
God will help her at dawn.

Nations tremble, and kingdoms shake.
God shouts, and the earth crumbles.
The Lord of heaven's armies is with us.
The God of Jacob is our protection.
Selah
Come and see what the Lord has done.
He has done amazing things on the earth.
He stops wars everywhere on the earth.
He breaks all bows and spears and burns up the chariots with fire.
God says, "Be still and know that I am God.
I will be praised in all the nations.
I will be praised throughout the earth."
~ Psalms 46:5-10

July 30

Dear God,

Lord, I hope we did the right thing.

People needed to know what was really going on. YBR was getting attacked by legions of trolls—Ripley named them the Flying Monkeys. They called us crazy conspiracists for making up stories that the white-haired Ragers got the Cure. They posted videos of people on their deathbeds getting *fused* and then walking out of the hospital completely healthy, even doing jumping jacks. They put up charts and graphs of statistics touting how effective the Cure is. They never report anything about the side effects, or the fatality rate. We were losing ground. We had to do something. So, we came up with a plan.

First, we had to apply for the Cure. Mason was the logical choice since he had a record and a history of drug abuse. He applied and got accepted within a few hours. He had to report to the Larkin Street Infusion Center in three days.

Ripley drove us to the center, a big office building on Larkin Street. He had rigged up a recorder thing for Mason to keep in his pocket. Ragers with guns and baseball bats surrounded the huge building like they were guarding it—that seemed weird. Mostly the Ragers just go around destroying stuff. They had dyed their white hair all sorts of wild colors, so it looked like a literal clown show. They wouldn't let us drive through—Mason had to go alone. I could tell he was nervous, but he acted like he was cool. I said a quick prayer over him, and then he kissed me, said he'd be back soon, and hopped out of the van.

Two Ragers met him at the barricade, demanded to see his QR Code, and walked him all the way to the entrance. They looked like giants next to Mason, but he walked tall and straight like he didn't have a care in the world. He was putting on a good show.

Two other Ragers motioned for us to leave—they looked like they meant business. Ripley drove the van a little farther away but stayed within sight of the entrance.

That's where we are now. This waiting is killing me. I'm praying hard and reading Psalm 91.

Those who live in the shelter of the Most High
will find rest in the shadow of the Almighty.
This I declare about the Lord :
He alone is my refuge, my place of safety;
he is my God, and I trust him.
For he will rescue you from every trap
and protect you from deadly disease.
He will cover you with his feathers.
He will shelter you with his wings.
His faithful promises are your armor and protection.
~ Psalms 91:1-4

I like the idea of You having feathers—it makes me smile. You as a gigantic mother bird who keeps us warm and safe in the shelter of your wings. Your promises are armor. That's badass.

Please, please, please rescue Mason from every trap. Amen.

July 31

Dear God,

Sorry I couldn't write more yesterday. Things went haywire.

We waited for two hours—no sign of Mason. I was getting really worried. He was only supposed to go in, talk to some people, and leave as quickly as he could. Something was wrong. Was it possible they'd forced him to go through with the procedure?

I was about ready to barge in those doors when he came bursting out, followed by a small crowd of people. Ragers joined in the chase—one of them tackled Mason. I screamed at Ripley to hit the gas. He drove right through the barricade. My heart was pounding so hard it made my ears hurt.

Mason somehow got free—he scrambled up and charged the van as we careened toward him. More Ragers converged on us, smashing bats and two-by-fours against the van, shattering two windows. Mason jumped onto the running board, holding onto the rear-view mirror as we raced away. I shrieked, "Lord, save him!" I know You heard me. I managed to get the sliding door open—how did I even do that?—so Mason could jump inside.

Once we got the door shut, Mason collapsed on the floor, so out of breath he couldn't say a word all the way home. I lay down next to him and held him in my arms until his breathing slowed.

As soon as we pulled into the underground garage, Mason jumped out, ran inside, and disappeared into his room, shutting the door behind him. He left the recording device on the coffee table.

I wanted to go in after him but decided against it. Mason doesn't like people to see him when he was upset. He's like a turtle ducking into his shell when things get too crazy. Instead, I picked up the recorder and handed it over to Ripley, who was pretty freaked out himself.

Ripley plugged the recording into his computer. Ralph and Miss Em came in to listen. Hearing it made me shake all over again.

Ripley made a transcript—I'm just going to include the important parts here.

[Sounds of people talking softly in the background, someone breathing, shifting around. This goes on a long time—obviously the waiting room]

MASON: You here for the Cure?

OTHER VOICE (barely audible) Yeah.

(Pause. More breathing.)

MASON: Do you…know anyone who's had it yet?

OTHER: My brother.

MASON: Oh? Cool. How was it?

OTHER: Uh…good. I think. I mean, at first, he was doing

great. He said it made him feel like Superman, almost, 'cause he couldn't get the virus or get sick with anything. He go running all the time and do pushups—that was weird, 'cause he never did stuff like that before. He used to be a couch potato. I thought maybe I should try it.

MASON: Wow. Awesome. How's he doing now? Your brother?

OTHER: Uh…I don't know. Haven't seen him in a while.

MASON: How come?

OTHER: He took off. Disappeared one day. Hasn't come back.

MASON: Was that strange?

OTHER: Yeah, I guess so. He didn't tell me. We used to be close, but…he kind of changed.

MASON: Oh yeah?

OTHER: One day I came home and found the kitchen all a mess—all the food pulled out of cupboards and thrown everywhere—eggs smashed against the walls. Garbage all over the floor. My mom about hit the ceiling. But we never saw my brother after that. My mom called the police, but they said they didn't have time to go looking for him. It was weird.

[Mason starts to ask another question but gets interrupted.]

FEMALE VOICE: Mason, we are ready for you now.

[Sounds of movement, footsteps, doors opening, a curtain being pulled]

NURSE: I just need to take your vitals and a blood sample before we begin the procedure. Sit on the table, please, and roll up your sleeves.

MASON: Will it hurt? The procedure?

NURSE: Not at all. Afterward, you may have severe headaches and body aches and be very fatigued for a few days. But then you will feel wonderful. Like a new person.

MASON: Have you had it?

NURSE: Me? No.

MASON: Why not?

NURSE: I'm not eligible yet. Hold out your arm, please.

MASON: How come? I mean, how come you aren't eligible?

NURSE: I don't make the rules. Hold out your arm.

MASON: Look, please, before I do this, tell me you think this is totally safe. 'Cause I'm a little scared.

NURSE: Why? You're going to be fine. Most people are.

MASON: Most people?

NURSE: Well…there are always some people that don't react well. They aren't compatible. It's true for any medication.

MASON: How do you know if you're…not compatible?

NURSE: Look, I'm not the one you should ask. I only do in-processing.

MASON: Who can I talk to, then?

NURSE: I don't know. (getting impatient) Let's just get your blood drawn, okay?

MASON: Just tell me this—can you die from it?

NURSE: From the procedure? Of course not.

MASON: So…no one has died?

NURSE: (long pause) Of course not. Not from the procedure.

MASON: But people *have* died?

NURSE: Will you please hold out your arm?

MASON: I just want to know—

NURSE: (impatient) Hold out your arm!

MASON: I think I changed my mind.

NURSE: You can't change your mind.

MASON: Why not? I just want to go.

NURSE: Look, stay here, I'll get someone to talk to you. You'll see—everything will be fine.

[Sound of door opening and closing. Mason's breathing. Footsteps. Door opening. More footsteps. Mason must have left the room and is walking somewhere. Muffled voices. Footsteps stop. It's a little hard to hear everything. Here's what we could make out.]

MAN: They are calling again, wanting a comment.

WOMAN: We have no comment.

MAN: More people are starting to notice. We can't keep this quiet forever.

WOMAN: Sure we can.

MAN: We should stop the treatments, at least until we know more [unintelligible]

WOMAN: We can't. Not until we've fulfilled the quota.

MAN: But these reports—look what's happening to these people—[unintelligible]

WOMAN: That isn't our fault. These people are homeless, drug addicts. It's to be expected. Fix the reports. The media will say whatever we tell them.

MAN: I hope you're right—Hey! What are you doing here?

MASON: Sorry—

WOMAN: Are you lost, young man?

MASON: Uh…I was looking for the bathroom—

OTHER VOICE, PROBABLY NURSE: Hey! What are you doing? I told you to wait!

WOMAN: Steve, call security.

NURSE: You need to come with me.

MASON: Hey, let me go. I just want to leave. I won't say anything—

MAN: Security, we have a 1019 in Room 214, 1019…

MASON: Let me go—

[Loud scuffling. Shouts. Heavy breathing. Running footsteps.]

MASON: Oh God… get me out of here… please… God… please…

[Tape abruptly cuts off]

How he got away was only by the grace of You.

Poor Mason. He was so scared. But he did it. Ripley's working on edits. He wants to get it posted today.

I love the LORD because he hears my requests for mercy.
I'll call out to him as long as I live, because he listens closely to me.
Death's ropes bound me; the distress of the grave found me—
I came face-to-face with trouble and grief.
So I called on the LORD 's name: "LORD, please save me!"
The LORD protects simple folk;
he saves me whenever I am brought down.
You, God, have delivered me from death,
my eyes from tears, and my foot from stumbling,
so I'll walk before the LORD in the land of the living.
~ Psalms 116:1-4,6,8-9

August 2

Dear God,

The video went viral. So far, it has almost a million views.

Mason still hasn't come out of his room. I'm worried about him.

Though I am surrounded by troubles,
you will protect me from the anger of my enemies.
You reach out your hand,
and the power of your right hand saves me.
~ Psalms 138:7

August 28

Dear God,

Mason is not himself.

He's barely talking or eating. He stays in his room almost all day.

I finally barged in this morning to talk to him, but he wasn't there. He must have gone out early.

I called his phone, but he didn't pick up. When he came home, he said he had trouble sleeping and went for a walk. He looked like he hadn't slept at all. His eyes had that weird pulse to them like they used to before he got saved.

Lord, I think he's using again.

How could he? He's been clean for so long.

Give me the courage to confront him. I know he's going to lie. Users always lie. But I can't let him destroy himself over this.

The Lord is my light and my salvation—
so why should I be afraid?
The Lord is my fortress,
protecting me from danger,
so why should I tremble?
My heart has heard you say,
"Come and talk with me."

And my heart responds,
"Lord, I am coming."
~ Psalms 27:1,8

September 5

Dear God,

Better today. Eyes are clear. He even joined us in the Hole while Ralph did a little sermon, and we sang some hymns.

Ralph talked about Your resurrection. What that must have been like, for Mary, as she walked to the tomb, eyes swollen from crying, to see the stone rolled away and...nothing there. She wasn't scared. Everyone else was scared, but not Mary Mags. She was curious. She had to *know*. I love that about her. She hung around, searching for You. She waited.

And yet when You showed up, she didn't recognize you. That always bothered me. How could she not? Maybe she didn't expect you to look human anymore. Paul said that our resurrected bodies won't look like our mortal bodies. So maybe you were just so different. You could have appeared as some great god, some mighty angel. Yet You looked so...ordinary. Like a gardener. A gardener! How perfect is that? You *were* a gardener, after all. The first.

Anyway, Mason and I took a walk after dinner. It was raining, just like on the day he proposed. But this rain just felt cold and miserable. I asked him how he was doing. He said he was fine but sounded mad, like he didn't like me asking. I let it be. But I'm still worried. I was hoping we'd talk about getting married again, but he didn't bring it up. Has he changed his mind? Doesn't he want me anymore? What does he want?

This is my prayer today:

Turn to me and have mercy,
for I am alone and in deep distress.
My problems go from bad to worse.
Oh, save me from them all!
Feel my pain and see my trouble.
Forgive all my sins.
~ Psalms 25:16-18

September 10

Dear God,

Mason hasn't come home for three days.

I thought he would come back eventually, like he always does. Looking disheveled, eyes all wild, smelling like you know what. But he comes home.

Not this time.

I've been out looking for him all day, checking out his old haunts. The seedy bars are open, even though the churches are still closed. No one answered at the auto shop.

Where did he go? Please, show me where he is. And please watch over him. Take care of him. Don't let him do something stupid.

I didn't realize how bad Buffalo had gotten until I walked the streets. The underpasses are like tent cities now. Trash everywhere. Seems like no one is picking up the garbage anymore. Drug addicts roam around like zombies, half dead. I kept my hoodie up and my hands in my pockets to avoid being accosted. Store windows are either broken or boarded. I couldn't get near Delaware Avenue because almost all of downtown has been taken over by Ragers—they've even put up barricades so cars can't get through.

Help me find him, please!

Commit your way to the LORD ! Trust him! He will act.
~ Psalms 37:5

September 12

Dear God,

I found him. In Silo City.

Why didn't I go there before? Silo City was where Mason lived when he was Mace, doing his Satanic stuff. I should have known he would go there to hide.

The place was overrun with homeless—whole families living in the silos, along with teens and young men stoned out of their minds. I went straight into Jared's Silo—that's what we called the one Jared lived in. Addicts called out to me as I passed by, asking for weed, for pills, for whatever I had to give. That was me, once, I thought. My world. Thank You for saving me from this.

A wild-haired guy jumped out of a cardboard box and followed me around as I searched for Mason, offering me the product he was peddling. Bath Salts, Candy, Brown Sugar, Krokodil, Party Powder—sounded like a grocery list. I told him I was looking for someone and described Mason. He clammed up, said he never saw no one like that. Said if I wasn't buying or using, I should get out. He tried to act all menacing, but I could have knocked him over with my little finger.

Then someone grabbed my arm. I spun around, ready for a fight. It was a teenage girl with pink hair and black-rimmed eyes, wearing a torn t-shirt that exposed most of her midriff. She said she knew who I was looking for and would show me, for money. I gave her a ten-dollar bill—she stuck it in her shirt and walked away. I followed her through more silo rooms until we came to one that was so dense with smoke, I could hardly see a thing.

There he was, curled up in a ball on a filthy blanket, asleep or so high he was barely conscious. His hair was greasy and crusted with what looked like vomit. Everyone around him was in the same condition. They smelled like a cesspit.

I went over and kicked him. I was so mad. He barely moved. I kicked him harder and yelled. Get up, you freaking idiot! I couldn't help myself. Finally, he started moving and groaning, and then the rage inside me broke and I started to cry. I fell on my knees next to him and cried and cried. He started crying too and babbled something about being sorry, and I just told him to shut up because I didn't want to hear it. I told him he was a loser and he better never do this again or I would kill him myself.

Somehow, I got him out of that place and into the car. He started blubbering about how he just didn't want to live anymore. Couldn't take it. The world. It was too much. Too hard. He was tired. He had no job, no life.

I told him he was an idiot. I told him I loved him. *You* loved him. That was enough. He couldn't give up and throw his life away and make everyone else miserable. We'd both tried that before and it didn't work.

Now comes the hard part. Withdrawal.

I need to apologize to him for my words. I didn't act right; I know it. I truly am sorry. Sometimes my temper gets the better of me. He is alive, and I am thankful for that. You led me to find him. I will apologize. As soon as he's in his right mind again.

I am under vows to you, my God;
I will present my thank offerings to you.
For you have delivered me from death
and my feet from stumbling,
that I may walk before God in the light of life.
~ Psalms 56:12-13

September 15

Dear God,

We made it to day three.

Thank You for getting us through this. For protecting us and for protecting Mason. We knew if things got bad, we couldn't take him to a hospital. He was on their list now. He could be arrested for what he did at the infusion center. We were on our own.

I stayed up all night with Mason for the first night, bathing him through the sweats and the chills and the vomiting, calming him down when the cravings got so bad, he actually tried to claw through the wall. He had hallucinations of snakes slithering out from under the bed and ants biting his skin and even I looked like a monster to him at times. I played this song over and over on Jared's old boom box—it seemed to help, though his limbs still jerked and twitched like an electric current ran through them.

When peace, like a river, attendeth my way,
When sorrows like sea billows roll;
Whatever my lot, Thou hast taught me to say
It is well, it is well with my soul.

I found a demo tape of Grace and Jared singing *Dragons* and played that for him too—he even sang along at times. We always thought that song was about us.

Dear God, won't you
Take me away to a place
Where the dragons don't watch us like birds of prey?
They sneak around to try and tear us down

But the dragons won't sleep until they've run us out of town.

He slept a few minutes at a time. Miss Em stocked his room with tea and aspirin, and the three of us gathered to pray over him each night. The fits have grown shorter. He no longer rages and swears, trying to climb out of his own skin.

This morning, Ripley actually got him into the shower. Miss Em grabbed his sheets and all the dirty clothes and hauled them off to the laundry room. I sprayed it all down with Lysol and air freshener and washed the floor. Trying to get rid of the smell—it's hard, being that we're underground.

When he's ready, I'll talk to him—apologize. Lord, give me the words to speak!

I rewrote this one in my own words:

I will listen to what God the Lord says;
but let me not turn to folly.
~ Psalms 85:8

September 15—later

Dear God,

Whew. That was rough.

After dinner—Mason actually ate some eggs and drank all his tea—I told him I was sorry for yelling at him and for not seeing sooner how messed up this whole thing had made him. He said he was sorry too. For letting me down. Letting all of us down. For being stupid. I didn't contradict him on that one. I've been there. I was stupid too. Gotta own up to it. Only way to change.

He said he just couldn't get past it. His life was going so good before. He had a job, he had me. A real life of his own. We were going to get married and maybe buy a house and have some kids and live happily ever after.

But then this virus, the lockdowns, losing his job—he lost himself. Then the thing at the infusion center—it was the last straw. Something broke in him, he said. He didn't see any reason to live. He thinks we're gonna lose this battle. There's too much against us.

I said maybe we will lose, but we will go down fighting. He

said he's not like me. He's not a fighter. I said, are you kidding? You've been fighting all your life. You're alive, aren't you? Not that many people live through what you've lived through. I reminded him of what Paul said:

We aren't fighting against human enemies
but against rulers, authorities, forces of cosmic darkness,
and spiritual powers of evil in the heavens.
Therefore, pick up the full armor of God
so that you can stand your ground on the evil day
and after you have done everything possible, to still stand.
~ Ephesians 6:11-13

I told him we're living that now. I think he heard me. Lord, I pray he heard me. He's got a lot to think about. A lot of healing to do.

Another re-write:

Have compassion on him, Lord, for he is weak.
Heal him, Lord, for his bones are in agony.
He is sick at heart.
How long, O Lord, until you restore him?
Return, O Lord, and rescue him.
Save him because of your unfailing love.
~ Psalms 6:2-4

December 25

Dear God,

We got married on Christmas Eve. In Silo City.

It was my idea, actually. Silo City had a lot of history for us. Plus, it was the only place the HASOs don't go.

Blaine started going there after I told him about Mason—it's like his new church now. He holds services a couple of times a week for the homeless and the addicts, and he hands out food and blankets. We've been going to help him as much as we can.

Mason wasn't too keen on returning to that place, but he came to see it as a way of reclaiming that ground, a kind of redemption. Silo City was just like us—forsaken, forgotten by the world. But not by God.

Of course, there was a white-out snowstorm yesterday. But the snow actually made Silo City—not the prettiest place for a wedding—kind of magical. As we walked down the concrete steps into Jared's Silo, I remembered the first time we came here, Grace, Bree, Ethan, and I, looking for Jared. We thought he was dead, but Grace had sworn she had heard him singing. We thought she was imagining things—turns out she wasn't.

We made our way through the clusters of homeless to the room that contained Silas' artwork—elaborate spray paintings of otherworldly creatures, aliens or angels. It was like having Silas there with us, in a way.

The place was packed with people and trash. We asked them if we could borrow their home for a wedding. To our surprise, they were thrilled. They cleared away all their stuff, so we had a place to stand. I'd brought the boom box to play the song Jared sang for Grace at their wedding. *Amazing Grace*, of course. Pretty soon, all those poor people were singing along. In that echo chamber, it sounded like—angels. I only wished that Grace and Jared were there, too.

I wore the only dress I own. It's purple and almost matches my hair. I didn't have any fancy shoes, so I wore my usual black boots. Mason wore a leather jacket that I'm pretty sure belonged to Jared—it was a little too big for him. Jared wouldn't mind. Ralph wore his professor's tweed coat, Miss Em wore a frilly pink dress under her lake-effect coat, and Ripley had on an enormous rust-colored puffy jacket that made him look like the Michelin man. Quite a wedding party.

I didn't wear a coat, and I was freezing. The silo was like a big stone castle, holding in the cold like a refrigerator. I shivered while Blaine said the words of the blessing, and we spoke our vows. Maybe it wasn't just the cold. I was shaking on the inside.

Because of what I was about to do.

Get married.

Yikes.

Mrs. Penny Watkins.

I still can't get over it. When I said those words, "I do," my heart thumped like crazy, and my head got so dizzy I thought I was going to faint. Here I was, marrying the guy who almost killed me. If that wasn't redemption, nothing was.

And seeing Mason's face—how happy he was. How full of joy, when once there was nothing but hate in him. How is it possible for a person to change like that? Only You could do that.

I feel guilty, being this happy. 'Cause the world is a dark place now. Israel is still under attack. Ragers have taken over many cities all over the world. The media calls them "New People", I guess because the Cure made them practically superhuman.

The government suddenly suspended the Cure program and is trying to deal with the problem of the New People, still claiming it has nothing to do with the Cure.

But I got married.

Do I have any right to be happy amid all this chaos?

I'm reading Psalm 118 today. I read once that it was Martin Luther's favorite. Days like today, it's mine too.

Oh give thanks to the Lord, for he is good;
for his steadfast love endures forever!
Out of my distress I called on the Lord;
the Lord answered me and set me free.
The Lord is on my side; I will not fear.
What can man do to me?
I shall not die, but I shall live,
and recount the deeds of the Lord.
~ Psalms 118:1,5-6,17

PS. Happy birthday, by the way. I know it's not your actual birthday but have a happy one anyway.

YEAR SEVEN

Grigori

YBR Podcast #50

Greetings from Kansas, Munchkins! Your Auntie Em here, as always.

There's a new thing happening in the faraway land of Scandinavia—it appears the Norse gods have been awakened by the savage fury of the New People. They've descended from the glaciers and ice floes of the fjords to take back the streets.

No doubt you have already seen the videos circulating the internet. Huge men with capes—capes! We haven't seen capes since the last Avengers movie. Over a hundred of them, white hair flowing in the breeze, led by a most spectacular one-eyed warrior riding a monstrous white horse. Their weapons are crystal spears and strange, circular bows that shoot electronic arrows like lightning bolts. New People surrender without a fight—they fall to their knees and raise their hands as if they have been waiting all along for their gods to appear.

We couldn't help but wonder: is this some elaborate publicity stunt? An Ozzie plot to ease the fears of a populace wearied by years of terror and isolation? The Lollipop Guild has been on the case, dissecting the videos for signs of deepfake tomfoolery. So far, they say, the videos look entirely genuine, backed up by phone videos of eyewitnesses who say even they can't believe their eyes. If this is fakery, it is fakery at the highest level. Could the Ozzies have some new tech so advanced that even our Guild cannot detect the swindle? Highly unlikely but not out of the realm of possibility.

The world is taking notice. The European Union has called upon the leader of this strange band of godlike warriors to help them with their New People problems. There may be a light at the end of the tunnel—we can only pray it isn't an oncoming train.

Meanwhile, the Alliance for Justice has taken over Tel Aviv. The lab where the virus was supposedly released is a ball of flame. Jerusalem is next on the menu.

Prime Minister David ben Judah has been on the air day and night, begging the UN and NATO to intervene. The UN quibbles about what to do and does nothing. NATO pays lip service to Israel as an ally of NATO, though not a member, while most of its members are supporting the Alliance. There is talk of nukes now.

Can these caped crusaders stop this apocalyptic train? More on them in the next podcast. In the meantime, remember the words of Jesus in John 8:32:

You shall know the truth. And the truth shall set you free.

Later, Munchkins.

February 3

Dear God,

They call themselves the Grigori.

Grigori. Greek for Watcher.

The Watchers have returned.

How did they get out of prison? Was it the collider accident? That's what Ripley thinks. Ralph said they would be released when the end was near. I guess that means we are there already.

Still, the collider accident was seven years ago. Why are they only appearing now? Maybe they needed time to get ready, to wait for the world to fall completely apart before they made their big move.

Mason and I started reading up on the prophecy to get a handle on what's been happening. This kind of blew our minds.

And the fifth angel blew his trumpet, and I saw a star fallen from heaven to earth, and he was given the key to the shaft of the Abyss. He opened the shaft of the Abyss, and from the shaft rose smoke like the smoke of a great furnace, and the sun and the air were darkened with the smoke from the shaft. Then from the smoke came locusts on the earth, and they were given power like the power of scorpions of the earth. They were told not to harm the grass of the earth or any green plant or any tree, but only those people who do not have the seal of God on their foreheads. They were allowed to torment them for five months, but not to kill them, and their torment was like the torment of a scorpion when it stings someone. And in those days people will seek death and will not find it. They will long to die, but death will flee from them.

~ (Rev 9:1-6)

We asked Ralph: who's the star fallen to earth who opened the Abyss? And who are these weird creatures that rose up like smoke, locusts with the power of scorpions—are those the Grigori? Are they tormenting the New People like scorpions? Or are the New People themselves the scorpions? It's true that the New People are mostly surrendering—the death tolls have been surprisingly low, but I figured that was just because New People are so hard to kill. But do they long for death?

There is a description of these creatures:

In appearance the locusts were like horses prepared for battle: on their heads were what looked like crowns of gold; their faces were like human faces, their hair like women's hair, and their teeth like lions' teeth; they had breastplates like breastplates of iron, and the noise of their wings was like the noise of many chariots with horses rushing into battle. They have tails and stings like scorpions, and their power to hurt people for five months is in their tails. They have as king over them the angel of the bottomless pit. His name in Hebrew is Abaddon, and in Greek he is called Apollyon.
~ *(Rev 9:7-11)*

It's hard to tell if this refers to the New People, who are basically Nephilim, or the Grigori. The Grigori do have human faces—very beautiful faces—and they have long white hair, like a woman's. They do wear breastplates like old-time warriors, and they have these fantastical flying cars that make a whirring noise— I suppose it could sound like many chariots going into battle. I mean, what would John have known about flying cars? It says their king is Abaddon—that gave me chills. Derrick called himself that. Abaddon, the destroyer.

The leader of the Grigori calls himself Grigori Zazel. Sounds a little like Azazel—Jared's father. Not his actual birth father, but his ancestral father. In the prophecy, there is a "the beast that rises from the Abyss." Sounds like Azazel. Man, this is so weird! And then Ralph told me to read another passage.

As I watched, the Lamb broke the first of the seven seals on the scroll. Then I heard one of the four living beings say with a voice like thunder, "Come!" I looked up and saw a white horse standing there. Its rider carried a bow, and a crown was placed on his head.

He rode out to win many battles and gain the victory.
~ *(Rev 6:1-2)*

That sounds like Jesus, I said. Ralph said, yes, it sounds like Jesus, but it isn't. Jesus will be riding a white horse, that's true, but he doesn't carry a bow, he carries a sword. This is a demonic imitator of Jesus. Look what follows: War, famine, disease, death. Not a sign that this is the real Jesus returned.

Zazel is for sure a superb imitator. People in Scandinavia call him their *savior*. They use that word a lot. *Savior*. Social media is blowing up over him. It is pretty amazing—in just a few weeks, he's completely stopped the Rages in Norway and Sweden. Now he's going to Finland.

Would someone—or thing—as evil as Azazel do something good like that?

This is really confusing. Lord, please help me understand.

I just want everything to go back to the way things were. I want to take a walk in the park without fear of drones or HASOs watching us. Mason and I gave up our phones because we found out they could track our movements and haul us to a quarantine camp if we came within proximity of an infected person. We bought some old-fashioned walkie-talkies online, but they don't have a very long range.

We go to Blaine's church services in Silo City a few times a week. He's getting quite a following. Some of them just want the free food and blankets we hand out. I pray they might hear something that will stick with them.

Guess who I ran into there. Mabel! Remember her? I didn't even recognize her at first, but she recognized me. She came right up to me and reminded me of the night I wrote my number on her arm. She never called it, she said, but she looked at that number on her hand a lot before it faded away. She ended up in Silo City to get away from the HASOs, but then she started listening to Blaine's sermons, and she wanted to meet this Jesus he was talking about. Next thing she knew, she was getting baptized!

I love how I can plant seeds, and You will make them grow.

Not that it's always easy. There's a lot of demon activity in Silo City. I met a girl named Anna yesterday. Right away, I sensed a spirit on that girl. She had long, ugly scars on her arms where she had cut herself repeatedly. I told her I could help her if she wanted to stop doing that. I thought she would refuse, but she nodded and started crying.

I told her to sit on a blanket on the floor and I got a few people who had accepted Christ along with Mason and Blaine to form a circle around her. Right away, Anna started hyperventilating. As we prayed, she shook and clawed at her arms with her fingernails. I asked a woman in the circle named Carrie to hold her hands so she couldn't hurt herself. I talked to the demon—what is your name? Ralph taught me that once a demon tells you its name, you can get control. The demon refused to answer. Anna started thrashing around so violently that Mason and Blaine had to help Carrie hold her down. Anna spewed all kinds of expletives as that demon manifested—she seemed to have the strength of a football player. It was all Mason and Blaine could do to keep her from reaching for my throat.

People gathered around to watch, some looking absolutely terrorized. I wasn't afraid—facing demons head-on just makes me really angry. I demanded the demon's name until Anna finally shouted, Hadad! I knew Hadad was another name for Ba'al. A pagan god in the Old Testament who commanded his followers to cut themselves with swords in worship.

I ordered that demon out of the girl in Your name. Anna started foaming at the mouth, her body jerking up and down so wildly I got worried she might really hurt herself or one of us. I held her head in my hands, ignoring the spit she hurled in my face, and told her to renounce the demon Hadad. Mason and Blaine kept up a steady stream of prayers while Carrie started singing: *It is Well with My Soul*. With a cry of total anguish, Anna finally screamed out the words. Then she went completely limp.

We all held our breath, gazing down at the suddenly motionless girl. Anna, I said. Anna, can you hear me? After a few minutes, she opened her eyes. And she smiled.

We baptized her right away after that, along with several other Silo City residents who suddenly wanted to be baptized. The air felt so different suddenly, despite the clutter and the smell of that place. We sang hymns of praise and prayed together and, for that short time at least, we were at peace. The demons had left the building.

I won't lie—these deliverances take everything out of me.

Thank You for giving me Mason—he is always there to support me. And thank you for Blaine and all the others who prayed for Anna. If You had to give me this difficult gift, I know You also gave me everything I need to use it.

This psalm reminds me of how awesome You are. How much You care for us, and for those stuck in Silo City, the Forbidden, the Forgotten.

Then they cried to the Lord in their trouble,
and he delivered them from their distress.
He made the storm be still,
and the waves of the sea were hushed.
Then they were glad that the waters were quiet,
and he brought them to their desired haven.
~ Psalms 107: 28-30

May 13

Dear God,

It's spring here in Buffalo, but you wouldn't know it. Yesterday we got an inch of snow. I think it's Mother's Day today. Not something I ever celebrated. I sometimes wonder if I will ever be a mother. I hope I do a better job than mine did.

Ripley showed us a video of the Grigori riding triumphantly through the streets of Helsinki, waving huge banners to cheering crowds. Like a Roman triumph, Ralph said. Complete with slaves—four hundred New People. They had their heads shaved and wore gray prison jumpsuits. The camera panned their faces. They didn't look defeated or shamed. Their eyes were on their new leader, Grigori Zazel. They looked...worshipful.

Mason thinks it's creepy. I have to agree.

How could the New People's violence magically turn to submission?

Ripley thinks the Cure contained nanobots that would allow the sending of wireless signals—that the New People are being controlled remotely. He says DARPA has been working on that kind of technology for years—mind control using sound waves—and that the behavior of the New People seems exactly like mind control. Sounds pretty far out to me. But who knows? A lot of Ripley's crazy ideas have come true. Nothing is too crazy anymore.

Zazel is going to bring his army to Europe to liberate the cities taken over by the New People. First Lady Shannon Snow-Ravel, Grace's mom, is going there to meet with Zazel personally. Because, of course, she is. She took one look at Zazel and decided she wanted a piece of that pie. And I'm betting not just for diplomatic reasons.

Sorry, Lord. That was mean. Sometimes I just can't help it. That woman still gets on my last nerve.

Zazel's face is on the screen 24/7 these days. You can't turn on a computer or television without seeing it. He's made for the screen; I have to admit. Prettier than most runway models, and so…*big*. What's with the eyepatch? Mason asked. Grace took his eye out in the Abyss, I said. I wonder why he didn't replace his eye with all the fancy tech he has.

Weirdly, the Rages in Buffalo seem to have subsided. Did the Grigori have something to do with that? Well, maybe things will calm down now and get back to normal. Forgive me, Lord, if I see some good news in all this madness.

Mason and I have decided to try and get an apartment of our own. I think it's time we left the Hobbit Hole. We love Ralph and Miss Em, but we feel like burdens to them what with their limited supplies. They can't even run the generator all day due to the fuel shortage. That's making Ripley nuts—he's used to staying up all night on his computers.

To be honest, it's getting a bit gloomy here. Ralph is still grieving for Jared and Grace—he hasn't told a dumb joke in ages. He hardly even laughs when Mason or I try to tell one. Miss Em does her best to keep up his spirits, but even she's starting to give up.

Despite all that's going on in the world, for the first time in a long time, I feel hopeful. Is that crazy? I'm not sure why. Maybe it's because things have got to get better, because they can't get any worse. Or maybe it's just that I trust You, and I know You won't abandon us. Ever.

I will exalt you, Lord, for you rescued me.
You refused to let my enemies triumph over me.
You brought me up from the grave, O Lord.

You kept me from falling into the pit of death.
Sing to the Lord, all you godly ones!
Praise his holy name.
For his anger lasts only a moment,
but his favor lasts a lifetime!
Weeping may last through the night,
but joy comes with the morning.
~ *Psalms 30:1,3-5*

May 15

Dear God,

Well, that hopeful feeling didn't last long.

Mason and I went looking for groceries for Miss Em today. The shelves were practically empty. Ravel says the shortages are only temporary, blaming the Rages, the virus, the war, and especially climate change. He's passed a bunch of new laws to fix the problems, though so far, they don't seem to be working.

We walked over to Elmwood, where we thought we would find a few smaller grocery stores still open. On the way, we were constantly accosted by homeless people doped up on drugs, which seem to be the only thing in this country that isn't in short supply.

As we passed a pharmacy, a group of masked teenagers burst out carrying garbage bags full of merchandise and ran down the street, hooting and hollering. They passed two cops standing on the corner. The cops didn't make a move to chase them. I was shocked. But Mason said shoplifting is legal now.

I spied a Korean grocery store across the street with crates of fresh fruit on display. My mouth watered—fresh fruit! Mangos and bananas. I grabbed Mason's hand and dragged him into the store. A Korean man and a woman, maybe his wife, were behind the counter, watching us warily. I smiled to let them know we wouldn't steal from them and laid two mangos and a bunch of bananas on the counter. I asked if they took cash. The man nodded. Relieved, I fished out some bills from my pocket.

Then I heard the woman shouting something and looked up to see a twenty-something guy and his girlfriend grab two big bunches of bananas and walk away. The shopkeeper abandoned me and ran over to the two thieves, demanding they pay. My pulse quickened—I squeezed Mason's arm. The guy's eyes roved wildly. His whole body shook. The girl started yelling at the shopkeeper, telling him to get out of her face, that they could take whatever they wanted.

I offered to pay for the bananas, but the shopkeeper ignored me. He stuck a finger in the man's face, still shouting in Korean. The thief grabbed the finger and bent it backwards, shoving the shopkeeper to the ground and falling on top of him. Bananas went flying. The wife screamed. Mason ran over to try to pull the crazed thief off the old man.

Then I saw the girl pull a knife from her bag. I yelled, "Knife!" Mason jumped away just as the girl came at him with the blade—she stuck him in the arm. Mason yelped in pain. I ran in and pushed her away. The knife flew out of her hand. She shrieked and started pummeling my head—she weighed about twice as much as me, so I didn't stand a chance. I tried to cover my head, but my vision was going all red and white and black. There was so much screaming and scuffling and grunting. Mason and the guy were still fighting, knocking over a display of mangos.

I cried Mason's name, though I could hardly see what was going on. Suddenly, the pummeling stopped—the girl ran away. I spun around to see the thief sprawled on the floor, the knife in his throat. His mouth worked like he was trying to speak.

Mason sat on his knees, head down almost to the floor, like he was praying. Blood from his arm soaked his sleeve. I asked him if he was all right. He just nodded. Started to cry. I held him. Blood trickled down my face. My head throbbed.

I felt a shadow, looked up to see the cop from the corner standing in the shop's doorway. I yelled, call an ambulance! Instead, the cop stepped over the body of the wounded man, grabbed hold of Mason's bloody arm, turned him over, and hand-cuffed him.

I screamed at the cop, told him it was self-defense, that the knife wasn't even his—the cop ignored me. He hauled Mason to his feet and dragged him out the door. A police car pulled up right outside, and the cop shoved Mason inside. They drove off.

I walked all the way to the police station, which looked more like a war zone: boarded up windows, graffiti on the walls, trash everywhere. I was told Mason had been taken to a quarantine camp. Why? I asked. Everyone goes there first to be cleared before they can be processed, came the answer.

I walked all the way to the quarantine camp, over ten blocks. They turned me away. No visitors.

I went back to the Hobbit Hole and told Ralph, Miss Em, and Ripley everything, between sobs. This can't be happening, I thought. My head still hurts so bad. I'm getting a black eye too. But I don't care about that.

Lord, please protect him in there. Please, please, please, get him out.

We need a miracle.

I rewrote this psalm, I hope you don't mind.

Turn to us, God, and have mercy on us
because we're alone and suffering.
Our heart's troubles keep getting bigger—
set us free from our distress!
Look at our suffering and trouble—
forgive all our sins!
Look at how many enemies we have
and how violently they hate us!
Please protect us! Deliver us!
Don't let us be put to shame
because we take refuge in you.
Let integrity and virtue guard us because we hope in you.
~ Psalms 25:16-21

May 17

Dear God,

Mason called today—they finally let him use the phone. He cried at first—he said he didn't mean to kill the guy. It was just that the guy went absolutely crazy on him. He didn't have a choice. He saw the knife on the floor and picked it up to keep it away from the thief, but then the thief charged him, ran right into the knife! No one at the camp would listen to his story. The cops didn't even interview the shopkeeper. The girlfriend was nowhere to be found.

The thief died at the hospital, probably because he didn't get treated in time. They charged Mason with murder.

Nothing makes sense anymore. The world is upside down. Lord, please help us. No one but you can give us justice.

How long, my Lord, will you watch this happen?
Rescue me from their attacks;
rescue my precious life from these predatory lions!
They don't speak the truth; instead,
they plot false accusations against innocent people in the land.
But you've seen it too, LORD. Don't keep quiet about it.
Please don't be far from me, my Lord.
Wake up!
Get up and do justice for me; argue my case, my Lord and my God!
Establish justice for me according to your righteousness, LORD, my
God.
Then my tongue will talk all about your righteousness;
it will talk about your praise all day long.
~ Psalms 35:17,19-24,27-28

May 25

Dear God,

I talked to Mason today. He said his arm still hurt from where he was stabbed, but otherwise he was okay. They tested him every day, and he was still negative for the virus, but they wouldn't let him leave the camp. It's more like a prison now.

He said he's been dreaming about the man's face—the man he killed. He killed people in his old life, and he'd asked for forgiveness, but now they are all coming back to haunt him. Maybe he's not really forgiven, he wondered. I told him he was—that You had washed away his sins—but I don't know if he believes that anymore.

Desmond—that's Ralph's lawyer— is working on getting him out. Ripley put out a video about the whole story, hoping that there will be a public outcry. Maybe it will help.

Lord, you forgave him, right? He's a different person now. He's turned his life around. He's confessed everything. Please don't let him suffer any more.

So I admitted my sin to you;
I didn't conceal my guilt.
"I'll confess my sins to the LORD," is what I said.
Then you removed the guilt of my sin. Selah
~ Psalms 32:5

July 15

Dear God,

Mason came home!

Thank You!

It was kind of a miracle. Desmond found out that the knife was engraved with the initials STN. So, he and Ripley scoured every engraving shop in the city until they found the one that had done the work. The owner even had a receipt with a woman's name. The girlfriend.

Desmond tracked her down and got her to admit that the knife belonged to her. That, combined with my testimony and the shop-keepers'—Desmond talked to them, the police never did because they "didn't have time"—forced the prosecutor to drop the charges. I'm angry that the cop who arrested Mason faced no discipline, but I'm learning to hand over these situations to You and let You deal with them.

Miss Em has been taking good care of Mason, stuffing him with meatloaf. Other than being tired and thinner, Mason says he feels fine. He said the camp was awful, and the guards tried to abuse him regularly, but he found he could keep them away by singing hymns really loudly. He just kept telling himself that after all he'd been through, this camp was nothing. There was one verse that he repeated all the time: The joy of the Lord is my strength. I'm so proud of him.

We're going to go on a picnic tomorrow, just him and me. He wants to sit somewhere outside where there are no walls or guards and breathe fresh air.

It's been a tough summer everywhere. A huge infestation of locusts destroyed acres of crops in the Midwest. California was hit by a mammoth earthquake that practically leveled San Francisco. There have been a record number of tornados throughout the Midwest. Fish in the Great Lakes are being gobbled up by slimy yellow sea lampreys which suck them dry like vampires. Extended droughts in the south have caused major crop failures. The Northeast has seen the emergence of a ravenous new insect that is stripping fruit trees and forests of foliage. The whole west has been engulfed in forest fires.

All over the world, stuff like this is happening. Much of the Middle East and North Africa are drowning in floods of "biblical proportions"; Russia was struck by several meteorites; a massive earthquake decimated Haiti; Iceland's volcanos are spewing ash over Northern Europe. They say the food shortages will only get worse because of all these so-called climate catastrophes.

I admit, I'm scared for the future. But today, I am happy, because Mason came home, and You did that.

I put all my hope in the LORD.
He leaned down to me;
he listened to my cry for help.
He lifted me out of the pit of death,
out of the mud and filth,
and set my feet on solid rock.
He steadied my legs.
He put a new song in my mouth,
a song of praise for our God.
Many people will learn of this and be amazed;
they will trust the LORD.
~ Psalms 40:1-3

YEAR EIGHT

Cure 2.0

YBR Podcast #80

Well, Munchkins, by now you have heard that a new Cure has arrived! While the Ozzies have yet to admit the untold damage caused by the previous Cure, they claim that Cure 2.0 is even more effective while being totally, completely, 100% safe. Did they take out the Nephilim DNA, we wonder? What did they replace it with? No one will say, but the government claims this one really, *really* works. And we should believe them because, you know, *science*.

The timing is rather curious —right in line with the Grigori suppression of the New People. By the way, that was quick, wasn't it? I mean, the caped crusaders have hardly touched down in Europe, but it seems as though the Rages all over the world have simultaneously ended.

How did that happen?

Did all the New People in the rest of the world stop raging merely out of fear? Or are they being controlled somehow?

We learned recently about a very interesting experiment that took place some twenty years ago. Project Pandora was the brainchild of a man named Amon H. Doyle, once an obscure scientist, now the chief advisor to William West, who calls him "A Prophet for the Next Age."

Project Pandora involved inserting very fine micro-wire electrodes—the diameter of a human hair—into the brain. Doyle's goal at the time was to tap into a person's brain activity and see what was going on. He called it "listening in to the music of the brain." We find that wording extremely interesting.

How far along did this experiment progress? We don't know, because Doyle, DARPA, and the Interlaken Group refuse to disclose the results of their experiments, or any data related to Project Pandora. It's classified. Top secret. We can only imagine.

Since then, Doyle has made quite a name for himself as a proponent of brain controlling Neurolinks and other fancy technology. These days, he trumpets a new kind of surveillance that goes "under the skin—inside the body." That is a direct quote.

Here are some more quotes from the Prophet himself, in case you wonder what he thinks of you.

[video clips]

"The biggest question is maybe in economics and politics of the coming decades, which will be what to do with all these useless people."

"What do we need so many humans for? We must keep them happy with drugs and computer games."

"Humans are hackable animals, without souls."

"We have the ability to upgrade humans into gods."

"The Fourth Industrial Revolution is about fusing our physical, biological, and digital identities so they cannot be separated."

"Just as God in the Bible designed creation to his wishes, we are learning how to create life. We are developing divine powers of creation and destruction."

[end of video]

When I hear this man being lauded by Ozzies all over the world, I can't help but think of Paul's words in First Corinthians: "Hasn't God made the wisdom of the world foolish?"

The New Cure, or THE FUSE, as President Harry Ravel likes to call it—such a catchy name, a *Harry* sort of name—will, according to the WHO and the CDC and every other acronym on the planet, end not only this pandemic but all pandemics yet to come. It's a literal miracle, just like the last one.

Forgive your Auntie Em if she doesn't believe everything the Ozzies say. I'm feeling somewhat skeptical these days.

And now they have thrown Darwin Speer under the bus—Speer, the creator of the OG Cure. The Ozzies blame Speer for the disasters that came from the Cure, even though they still won't admit there were any adverse side effects at all. The OG Cure, in fact, continues to be used in certain segments of the population—the military, the police, or I should say Peacemakers, as we don't use the term *police* anymore. It makes people uncomfortable. Peacemakers don't arrest criminals. They just make sure we are complying with the new rules "to ensure the peace and safety of all." That's their motto.

Well, Speer might have deserved it, and he is not here to defend himself. Len Wilder, his chief medical officer, the media's darling not that long ago—why there were bobbleheads and tea towels featuring his handsome face—has been hauled before a tribunal, charged with medical treason! The heroes are now the villains. It's a tale as old as time.

I am sure many of you will celebrate the arrival of this new Cure. Those of you who have spent the last several years locked in closets—between the virus and the Rages, it's no wonder. Those of you who have lost jobs and friends and family members and futures. There is a light at the end of the tunnel, you think! Grigori Zazel was declared the Premier of the new Scandinavian Union and has promised to work for a permanent peace between Israel and the Alliance. He's managed to engineer a temporary cease-fire. In Jerusalem, they dance in the streets, singing songs to their new savior, Grigori Zazel. Well, some of them are, anyway. The wiser ones are wary of wolves in sheep's clothing, to quote the "outdated and debunked" Good Book. And we here in Kansas are pretty certain that the shining, glorious Grigori Zazel is one hundred percent wolf.

Remember, there are two kinds of peace. Peace through freedom, as our nation has enjoyed for centuries. And peace through total and unmitigated control. Totalitarian regimes are built on *that* kind of peace.

Which kind do you think the Grigori will bring? The Interlaken Group? Our own President Harry Ravel and his wife, the former horror movie queen?

Something to ponder.

March 5

Dear God,

Sorry, it's been a while since I've been able to sit down and write. I'm so tired. Working all day at the restaurant and trying to fix up the apartment—it's a lot. By the end of the day, I'm so beat I just fall into bed and sleep. That's not an excuse, it's just—well, You understand, right?

I have the day off—snowstorm. Eighteen inches so far, and it's still coming down. They are calling it the "Storm of the Century." Four more feet are expected. The roads haven't been plowed. In fact, they rarely get plowed anymore. Buffalo used to be so good at stuff like that.

I don't mind waitressing. I thought people would really get on my nerves, but I like talking to them, just *seeing* people. They can take off their masks when they sit down, so I can see faces too. That's been nice. I miss faces.

The apartment is coming along. Mason and I are doing the repairs ourselves, learning as we go. Miss Em has come over with casseroles and decorating advice, although I'm not sure I'm going to take it—the advice, I mean, not the casseroles. The place was a wreck when we moved in, but it was cheap. Big holes in the walls and floors, like the previous tenants spent all their time throwing axes around. Maybe New People lived there—we can't call them Ragers anymore because that is considered discrimination.

There used to be a barbershop on the first floor. Now it's just a hangout for druggies. I mean, UPs, which stands for Un-Privileged, another new term we are supposed to use. One of the girls there has a mangy-looking terrier she calls Timmy. Those two make me feel sad whenever I see them. The girl can't be over eighteen. She probably won't make it to twenty, the way she's going. But she really loves that dog, which is nice, because that is the most unlovable dog I've ever seen. It's got bald patches and one ear looks as though it was bitten off in a fight. Its eyes are rheumy—it must be pretty old. I'm glad those two have each other.

The UPs are always begging us for money, which we don't have, so I bring them leftovers from the restaurant—day-old rolls and Danish, whatever is going to get tossed, which isn't much these days. I tell them about You too—they don't want to hear any of that, but I figure if they are gonna take the free bread, they should hear about the Bread of Life, right? Now whenever they see me coming, they start shouting, "Here comes the Jesus Girl! Saint Penny!" and they get on their knees and start bowing and doing the signs of the cross—all to make fun of me. I've had worse. When You were hanging on the cross, You forgave all those people who were making fun of You because they didn't know what they were doing. They were fools, just like these folks here. I know You'll forgive them. too.

Allentown used to be the hippest part of town, with lots of artist types and cute coffee shops. It's pretty torn up still, but people are out cleaning up the messes and putting their lives back together. It's pretty weird how the New People seem to have disappeared. Where did they go?

Mason is working at an auto shop on the outskirts of town. There are very few auto shops left that work on gas vehicles, and he wasn't trained on electric cars. He has to take a bus every day, so he leaves early in the morning and doesn't get back until after dark. Neither of us makes very much, and everything is crazy expensive. I went to a grocery store yesterday—the shelves are still mostly empty. Five dollars for a quart of milk. I bought a loaf of bread and peanut butter. We'll live on that this week.

Meanwhile, the government is paying people two thousand dollars to get the FUSE. I guess people are scared to get it because of what happened with the old Cure. Still, two grand is a lot of money. Everyone needs the cash. The news says there's another variant coming. This must be the fifth wave—I've lost count. I wonder if I'll get it this time since I'm working now. Ripley gave us some medicine he got through his underground channels that was banned by the government. They've even put doctors who prescribed it in jail, saying the medicine is dangerous and doesn't work. The FUSE is the only thing that works, they say. I don't know who to believe anymore.

I'm still hopeful that things are going to get better despite what Ralph and Ripley say. They could be wrong, after all. I just have to believe that the worst is behind us. That there's still a way forward. There's hope. After all, whenever one of your prophets would finish their doom and gloom predictions, they would promise a future restoration, a time when all would be well. Like Isaiah…I love this part. Didn't You say this was what You came to do? And why You will come back?

The Spirit of the Sovereign Lord is upon me,
for the Lord has anointed me to bring good news to the poor.
He has sent me to comfort the brokenhearted
and to proclaim that captives will be released and prisoners will be freed.
They will rebuild the ancient ruins, repairing cities destroyed long ago.
They will revive them, though they have been deserted for many generations.
Instead of shame and dishonor, you will enjoy a double share of

honor.
You will possess a double portion of prosperity in your land, and ev-
erlasting joy will be yours. "For I, the Lord, love justice. I hate rob-
bery and wrongdoing.
I will faithfully reward my people for their suffering
and make an everlasting covenant with them.
The Sovereign Lord will show his justice to the nations of the world.
Everyone will praise him! His righteousness will be like a
garden in early spring, with plants springing up everywhere.
~ Isaiah 61:1,4,7-8,11

September 20

Dear God,

Fired.

Mason too.

At least I'll have more time to journal.

It's because we didn't get FUSED. It used to be voluntary, until a month ago when Congress passed a law mandating every person in the country had to "Get FUSED" in order to work in any job, go to school, eat in a restaurant, shop in a store, or travel on public transportation.

You couldn't go anywhere without seeing that on billboards, on doorways, and on every website you opened. Ravel was on television four or five times a day talking about how we all needed to "Get FUSED now! Don't be a Re-FUSER!" Everyone from social media influencers to late-night comedy show hosts called Re-FUSERs either stupid or evil.

Mason and I both had already gotten the latest variant of the virus in the summer. We were sick for a week with a fever, nausea, and rashes, but we took Ripley's medicine, did oatmeal baths, and drank lots of Miss Em's tea, and we got better. My boss said I still had to get FUSED, even though I already had the virus. There were more viruses coming, she said. Variants of variants. This pandemic wasn't over—it would never be over. The Cure was the only way to be safe.

I said no.

I'm not even sure why. Maybe because they are trying to force me to take it, and that rubs me the wrong way. So far, the New Cure doesn't seem as bad as the old one, even though the CDC refuses to release any safety data. Ripley's got his hackers trying to find out what's in the New Cure. So far, Speeracles won't disclose any of the ingredients. They don't have to, he says, because the Cure is still under Emergency Authorization.

We can't afford our apartment now, so we have to leave. It was just getting to look cute, too. Allentown was almost pretty this summer, with people putting flowers in window boxes and setting out water bowls for passing dogs. Shops were opening again. Musicians played on street corners, just like in the old days, and the Bubble Man—this old guy who blew bubbles out of his window—was out nearly every day. I really thought everything was going to be okay.

Then yesterday, something awful happened. Big blue vans pulled up in front of our building, and HASOs got out, along with people wearing blue uniforms, masks, and face shields. Peacemakers. I thought they were coming for us, so I quickly locked the door and shouted for Mason. By the time he came to the window, the officers had gone into the old barbershop below and pulled out the UPs, dragging them into the van. The UPs fought back, screaming and kicking, but they were no match for the Peacemakers, who were all New People. I had to cover my ears from the screaming.

The girl resisted—she wouldn't let go of Timmy. Finally, a Peacemaker ripped the dog from her arms and threw her into the van. Another one slammed the door. And then...I almost can't write this...the Peacemaker took out a stick and beat that little dog to death. Right there on the sidewalk.

As long as I live, I will never get that sight out of my mind.

This place is cursed, I think. This world is cursed.

We're going back to the Hobbit Hole. We need to be with our family.

Let all that I am wait quietly before God,
for my hope is in him.
He alone is my rock and my salvation,
my fortress where I will not be shaken.
~ Psalms 62:5-6

Chips
YBR Podcast #83

Greetings from Kansas, Munchkins. Auntie Em here. I know you're worried. The WWW is back in town, and she's very angry. The misinformation is getting on her nerves. She's cracking down on all of us, so we don't know how much longer we can come to you through any of our current channels. Many of our videos disappear as soon as we post them, with no explanation. Our other platforms have been shut down as well. The WWW is pretty powerful. We will do our best to keep bringing you the news from Oz until the very end.

Remember when the Ozzies told you that life would return to normal if you got FUSED? Many of you believed them. You got the Cure. Some of you suffered severe side effects. Some even died. But everyone was safer because you did your part as a good citizen.

Then the Ozzies announced that you would have to get FUSED every three months for the rest of your life to maintain your immunity. The virus, you see, keeps mutating, and the Cure seems to wear off after a few months. Again, you complied. You dutifully carried your Cure-Pass with you wherever you went, so you could prove to every shopkeeper and maître d that you were doing your part to save humanity.

Unfortunately, the Cure-Passes became too easy to fake. The Ozzies needed a better way of keeping track of you and ensuring you were getting your boosters on time. And of weeding out the Re-FUSERs.

So now they have introduced the next phase of the plan: the Chip. We warned you about this. You called us conspiracy nuts. You said they would never require people to be chipped in order to live like normal people.

Sorry, Munchkins.

Let's hear it from Head Ozzie Ravel's own mouth.

[VIDEO OF PRESIDENT RAVEL SPEAKING FROM THE NATIONAL CATHEDRAL IN WASHINGTON DC]

"My fellow Americans, we've come so far together to beat back this terrible virus that has claimed so many lives. We just have a little bit farther to go. You've done your patriotic duty; you've gotten FUSED—well, most of you anyway—with the knowledge that not only are you protecting your own lives, but the lives of your fellow citizens, your family, and your friends as well. You are heroes, all of you who have played by the rules and complied with what your country has asked of you. Moreover, you've done what God wants you to do. God gave us the Cure so we would live! It was our Christian duty to get FUSED and to make sure all of our family and friends did too.

"But now, we have to ask one more thing. That you go down to the local implanting office—they are being established all over this great country—and have a tiny chip inserted into your hand, no bigger than a grain of rice. This way, you won't have to carry around a Cure-Pass anymore. The best part is that the chip will alert you—and your doctor—when it is time for your booster, so you will never be caught unprotected. To make it easier, everyone who gets their chip between now and the end of the year will receive a $1000 bonus check from the government. Isn't that great? The bonus check will decrease the longer you wait, so don't!

Get your chip now! You will love the convenience of it. And you will no longer have to worry about being unprotected. Friends, this is truly a great time to be alive. I know you will do the right thing for yourselves, your family, your country, and your world. God bless you all. And remember, don't be discouraged, and don't lose hope. Just keep on keeping on."

Keep on, keeping on. Some of us here in Kansas remember when he used to say that back when he was the pastor of that mega-church in California. Some things never change.

What should you do? When do you draw a line in the sand and say, no more?

Now is the time to choose.

We're praying for you.

YEAR NINE

The Rez

January 1

Dear God,

New Year's Resolution. Journal more often.

Not that I haven't been praying. It seems like all I do is pray these days. And ask You for help.

Are you listening?

For a while, I prayed that You would have mercy and spare us. Now, I pray that Your judgment will not destroy us. Because I'm pretty sure that our world is under judgment. Like it says in Romans, *You have abandoned this world to its own desires*. That's what I think, anyway.

There's been such a change since they started putting chips in people. First, they were paying people to do it—now they are punishing those who refuse. You can no longer work in the school system or any public job without a chip. You can no longer get a driver's license or a passport. Ripley says that pretty soon, we may not even be able to use the Internet. I can't understand that—no one is spreading the virus through the Internet. It's not about that, Ripley said. It's about control.

The Ozzies have launched a massive ad campaign to sell the chips. The New Cure is working great, they say. No one is worried about getting sick anymore. It's the Re-FUSERs who are the dangerous ones—the Re-FUSERs put everyone at risk by keeping the virus alive. Hospitals turn away Re-FUSERs, even if they don't have the virus. The only place Re-FUSERs can go for medical treatment is a quarantine camp. It's part of Ravel's new "REFUSE THE REFUSERS" campaign. He's a great one for catchy slogans.

Everywhere I walk, there are posters and billboards of smiling people—including children—holding up their hands to show off their new chips which glow when you hold your phone or a scanner over them. Ripley says they are embedded with a Luciferase enzyme that makes them glow when activated. What a name.

At first, there were protests and demonstrations against the chip law all over the country. But Peacemakers put an end to them with tear gas, water cannons, trained dogs, and new long range acoustic devices that caused many protesters to go deaf. So many people were injured and killed that Ravel suspended the right to protest in the interests of public safety. Everything these days is for public safety.

I've begged Ralph to move some place safer—some states seem to be resisting the new rules against Re-FUSERs. What if one of us got really sick? We can't go to a hospital and going to a quarantine camp would be worse than death. Still, Ralph is adamant that we stay. He says when You want him to move, You will tell him so.

Lord, I just don't know if that's true. I think there's something else going on with Ralph. It's almost as if he doesn't care anymore. Maybe he's given up.

In the meantime, what am I supposed to do here? If we really are meant to stay here, what can I do to help anyone or change anything? I'd really love to know. Please show me something. Because right now, it seems like you are letting the bad guys win.

How long will you hand down unjust decisions
by favoring the wicked?
"Give justice to the poor and the orphan;
uphold the rights of the oppressed and the destitute.
Rescue the poor and helpless;
deliver them from the grasp of evil people.
But these oppressors know nothing;
they are so ignorant!
They wander about in darkness,
while the whole world is shaken to the core.
Rise up, O God, and judge the earth,
for all the nations belong to you.
~ Psalms 82:2-5,8

March 14

Dear God,

We were glued to the computer all day, watching Grigori Zazel perform at the UN General Assembly. That's what it was, a performance, Oscar-worthy, in my opinion. He was so huge that he dwarfed everyone else on the stage except his Grigori warriors, who stood around him like golden statues. With his shining armor and silver hair all done in braids, Zazel looked like a superhero from the movies, like Thor or Superman.

He spoke for almost three hours, but unlike most other nutty world leaders, he had the audience enthralled. Or maybe they were terrified. The chamber erupted in applause every thirty seconds. Even I felt sucked into his strange magic. What did he say, exactly? A lot of talk about peace and brotherly love. An end to war and famine and pollution and climate change and disease. A perfect world.

I asked Ralph—could Zazel be the Antichrist? The Man of Lawlessness Paul and John and Daniel spoke of? Ralph wasn't sure. Zazel did fit a lot of the criteria, but there was nothing in the scriptures to say that the Antichrist would be a Watcher.

At any rate, it's clear that Grigori Zazel is taking over the world. There's nothing to stop him.

Except You.

I need a word of reassurance today. A word that reminds me You are in control.

But the Lord is in his holy Temple;
the Lord still rules from heaven.
He watches everyone closely,
examining every person on earth.
The Lord examines both the righteous and the wicked.
He hates those who love violence.
He will rain down blazing coals and burning sulfur on the wicked,
punishing them with scorching winds.
For the righteous Lord loves justice.
The virtuous will see his face.
~ Psalms 11:4-7

YBR Podcast #90

Greetings from Kansas, Munchkins. This will be our last transmission for a while. The Ozzies have kicked us off the internet by successfully lobbying ISPs and network administrators to block any channels deemed subversive, including YBR. We've been scrambling to find an ISP willing to stand up to the censorship, but so far, we haven't found one. The Ozzies have already put out a statement saying that soon all internet users will be required to register for a Digital ID, which of course, can only be obtained with a chip. Therefore, we knew our time was short.

We are working on other means of communication. Now's the time to get your shortwave radio out of the attic and fire it up.

We thought we would spend this last time together preparing you for what is coming. Is Grigori Zazel who we think he might be? Clearly, he bears a strong resemblance to one or more of the prophesied beasts, but which one? We don't know that yet, and we refuse to jump to conclusions. A lot must happen before we can be certain.

But there are signs. Zazel has brought peace by stopping the Ragers and cutting off support for the war against Israel. The EU is no longer sending cash and guns to the Alliance. Russia has turned its attention to annexing Ukraine and the Balkans. And China? China has already reaped the rewards of the war by expanding its control over most of Asia and increasing its wealth a thousandfold through the sale of PPE, microchips, and rare metals.

That leaves the core of the Alliance to soldier on alone. We give them nine months at most. Israel's Iron Dome and David's Sling missile defense systems have kept Jerusalem from turning to rubble, though the people inside the city are trapped and will soon be starving. David ben Judah makes daily appeals to "Let His People Go" and has expressed a desire to meet with Zazel personally. Zazel has so far ignored him.

He has not ignored a request from the Pope, however, and plans to go to Rome in a few weeks. The Pope speaks of Grigori Zazel as "the man who will save the world." Interesting choice of words, no? We'd love to be a fly on the wall when those two meet.

In case you missed Zazel's UN speech, it is being played *ad nauseum* on all channels and platforms these days. The great composer Roger Wainright is reportedly writing a new opera about him. Movie studios are falling over each other to license his story for a new superhero franchise. Dreamy-eyed teenage girls recite poems about him on TikTok. Kellogg's has named a cereal after him: Grigori Granola. Breakfast of Saviors. Lord, have mercy on us.

April 7

Dear God,

We're offline for good now.

I never thought it would happen, that they would actually kick us off the internet. It's a whole new world, as Ralph likes to say. I guess we're okay for now. Ralph and Miss Em have always been preppers, and we have our own generator, as long as we can get fuel. Ralph converted most of his assets to gold a long time ago. We have a few sources that still accept cash for some supplies, but I'm not sure how long that will last. Water is rationed, so we can only take showers every third day.

Otherwise, it's been quiet here. Ripley's been holed up in the Lair, trying to build a shortwave radio out of all the electronic junk he keeps in there. Ralph's engrossed in piles of books and scholarly papers, researching the Antichrist. Miss Em is worried about him—I can tell by the number of times a day she brings him tea and macaroons. At least he seems to be out of his funk for the time being. Silver lining.

I go out every day to rummage for newspapers in trash cans or walk down to the train station to find out what's happening in the world. Shannon was on TV with Zazel last week, gripping his muscular arm as she waved to the cameras from the top of the Eiffel Tower, the wind whipping their hair around their faces. They both looked absolutely stunning, despite the wind. I wondered if Harry was watching. He had to be thinking what everyone else in the world was thinking: Shannon has found herself a new man.

She had her kid with her, too. He's about nine now, I guess. His name is Wolf. Can you believe that? She claims she named him after one of her bad vampire movies. A cute little kid with Shannon's bright red hair, though his eyes are crystal blue. Grace's little brother. Too bad she never got to meet him. Bet she always wanted a little brother named Wolf. Doesn't everyone?

Times like this, I really miss Grace. Has it been nine years since she's been gone? I miss having a friend who's a girl. I could call Bree—we kind of lost touch after Grace went missing. Bree and Ethan got married in New York City—they sent me an invitation to the wedding, but I didn't go. I sent her an email when Mason and I got married, but she never wrote back. Maybe she moved.

Mason works most days and a lot of nights, fixing cars for people who don't ask him about his FUSED status. They don't pay very much. When he comes home, he's usually too tired to talk and just goes to sleep.

I'm lonely.

Why, my soul, are you downcast?
Why so disturbed within me?
Put your hope in God,
for I will yet praise him, my Savior and my God.
~ Psalms 42:11

May 15

Dear God,

Last night we woke up to loud knocking—we all freaked out because no one is supposed to know where we live. The Hole is under the burned-out Mansion, and the entrance is pretty well hidden. The surveillance system was off because we didn't have enough juice to keep the generator running all night. We thought for sure Peacemakers had come for us.

When Ripley turned on the video monitor, he saw the intruder was a friend of his, one of the Lollipop Guild named Stubby. Ripley let him in because he was making such a fuss out there, someone might have heard him.

Stubby was a wreck. He's an older guy with a really long beard, like most cellar-dwellers these days. I wonder why he's called Stubby—he's not particularly short. I don't know how he found us—Ripley swears he never told anyone where we lived. He had mentioned the Mansion, though, and Stubby said he remembered the burnt house from his old job as a mail carrier years before.

Once he'd calmed down enough to talk, he told us his story. He and a couple of Guild members he lived with had found a way around the internet blockades and were running a website where they posted evidence that the virus didn't come from Israel after all but from a virology lab in China funded by the Interlaken Group. Little did they know that their internet workaround was an Ozzie trap—Peacemakers raided their house in the middle of the night.

They swarmed the place in seconds, Stubby said. He only escaped because he'd gotten up to go to the bathroom. When he heard the commotion, he climbed out the window and jumped to the fire escape. It was the most athletic thing he'd ever done in his life, and he thought he would fall to his death. He thinks they took his friends to the quarantine camp.

Mason got kind of upset, saying Stubby could have led the Peacemakers straight to us. Stubby promised he'd been careful. What about drones? What about surveillance cameras? Mason's face turned all shades of red. I took him aside and told him to calm down. What was done is done. The Peacemakers hadn't shown up yet, so they probably wouldn't.

Ralph said Stubby could stay as long as he wanted, and Miss Em made him some hot chocolate. Ripley found an old sleeping bag, one of his Star Wars collection, and got Stubby set up in the Lair. Mason stalked off to our room, still angry. What are we going to do with him? he asked.

That got me thinking. What *are* we going to do?

I have no idea. But maybe You do.

Show me the right path, O Lord
point out the road for me to follow.
Lead me by your truth and teach me,
for you are the God who saves me.
All day long I put my hope in you.
~ Psalms 25:4-5

June 10

Dear God,

I think I know what You want me to do.

I got the idea while watching Stubby help Ripley get the radio working. Stubby turned out to be a radio genius—he said he grew up building radios with his dad and even had an FCC license. The two of them installed a giant antenna above ground, partially hidden by the old chimney of the Mansion, the tallest part of the ruin.

Within a week, Stubby had the YBR up and running as a radio station.

Soon they were talking to people all over the world. Since there wasn't much else to do, we all gathered around to listen to these conversations, which were mostly boring. These ham radio types sure love to talk! But one night, Rip and Stubby contacted a guy who lives on the Black Hills Reservation in South Dakota. He goes by the name Red Cloud.

He was a lot more interesting because he talked about life on the reservation, which was always hard but had gotten a lot harder since the virus. The internet on the Rez was pretty sporadic, so Red Cloud played around with radios and even worked for a communications company in Rapid City. He said his friends made fun of him for working and not drinking—he stopped drinking when he became a Christian. Those two things were considered marks of shame, apparently.

Red Cloud also mentioned that the tribal council was trying to attract more people to the reservation by having open enrollment, meaning you didn't have to prove you were an Indian to live there. Many people ended up on the Rez to escape federal prosecution because it was sovereign territory.

That's what got me thinking—the reservation was like a safe haven. What if Stubby went there?

I told my idea to Rip, who asked Red Cloud, who presented the idea to the tribal council. A few days later, he came back on the radio to say that while there was some opposition, the council voted to let Stubby come, provided he could get their radio station up and running.

Mason and I made plans to drive Stubby there ourselves. Ralph was against the idea—we'd have to go past Chicago. What if they were checking chips at the borders? What if there were drones? How would we find gas stations? Many of them had shut down completely.

Ralph has changed so much. This was the same guy who let Jared and Grace go into the Abyss? Who took on demons left and right without breaking a sweat? It's almost like they were getting the better of him.

We spent several days working out details, mapping out routes, and planning for contingencies. Since it was more fuel efficient, we'd take the Mini and carry some extra gas cans. In the end, Ralph consented and even gave us some gold bars to get Stubby set up on the Rez.

We're really doing this. Now that it's all settled, I'm having second thoughts. Is this the craziest thing we've ever done? What if the car breaks down? What if the Peacemakers stop us? What if we get lost? So many what-ifs.

Had to rewrite this one just for me...

I look up to the mountains—does my help come from there?
My help comes from the Lord, who made heaven and earth!
He will not let me stumble; the one who watches over me will not
slumber.
The Lord keeps me from all harm and watches over my life.
The Lord keeps watch over me as I come and go, both now and for-
ever.
~ Psalms 121:1-3,7-8

July 2

Dear God,

We made it to the Mississippi River. I've never seen a river other than the Buffalo River, which isn't very wide. This one is massive. Mason says we should cross at night to avoid drones.

Once we are out of Illinois, I will breathe a lot easier. Going past Chicago was nerve-wracking. Even though we stayed pretty far to the south of the city, I kept looking out the window, sure I saw the blinking lights of drones. We played worship music on the Mini's ancient cassette deck and prayed for invisibility.

My legs were half asleep, cramped up in the back seat of the Mini with the spare parts, gas cans, and assorted gizmos. I volunteered since I was the shortest. Stubby did the navigating with a wrinkled paper map because we couldn't use any kind of GPS. We got lost a dozen times. The gas fumes made me nauseous, not to mention Mason's driving. Stubby called him "Mason Andretti" for some reason.

Mason found a wooded area behind an old church to hide the car so we could get a few hours' sleep. It was one of those plain, clapboard churches you see on lonely country roads, but it looked like it had had a fire. There was a big hole in the roof, and the interior walls were charred. We ate the peanut butter sandwiches Miss Em had packed for us, and soon, Mason and Stubby were snoring away, stretched out on the pews. Boys. They can sleep anywhere.

I'm having a hard time getting to sleep. It's daytime, for one thing. Plus, we're probably trespassing and might get discovered. Also, the pews are really uncomfortable. I used to sleep under bridges and in doorways if I had to. This trip has made me realize that I'm not so young anymore. So, I'm catching up on my journaling instead. Maybe that will make me sleepy.

So far, we haven't run into any trouble, and there hasn't been much traffic. We stopped at three gas stations before we found one that had fuel and would let us pay in cash—they charged us double. Whatever…we paid. Their snack shelves were mostly empty except for a box of expired Twinkies, which we bought because Twinkies never really expire. At least the Mini is holding up, though there is a big hole in the floor, so I just pray we don't end up going through any puddles.

The smaller towns we've driven through seem pretty empty—businesses boarded up, restaurants permanently closed. Hardly any cars in the parking lots. Stubby said the towns are dying because people are moving to city centers just to get jobs and basic services. That seems really sad to me.

Stubby talked the whole ride—we couldn't shut him up once he got going. He told us why he's called Stubby. His name is Stuart, but his little sister couldn't pronounce Stuart, so she called him Stubby, and the name stuck. He tried getting his friends to call him Stu, but it never happened. Even his parents called him Stubby. He hated it at first, but he's gotten used to it, and it reminds him of his little sister, who was killed by a New Person during the Rages.

Stubby talked a lot about the Grigori. He thinks they are aliens, because of their impressive physiques and technological advancements. They've created a flying car that works without wings or rotors and recharges itself with kinetic energy. Their weaponry is like something out of a Marvel movie.

Stubby said Zazel is building a gigantic tower fortress on a mountain near Oslo, which he now calls New Asgard. It's over a hundred stories tall, and the top of it opens up to a crown of ten spires encircling a lush garden. It's a miracle of architectural engineering, according to Stubby. And it's being built five times faster than an average skyscraper.

I asked Stubby if he thought Grigori Zazel was the Antichrist. He kind of laughed like he thought I was joking. Isn't the Antichrist just a fairy tale? He asked. But you believe he could be an alien? I asked. To Stubby, the alien theory was more plausible.

Mason and I told Stubby our stories, how we came to know You, and how we know You're real. We also told him of all the prophecies and how they seemed to be fulfilled with the coming of the Grigori. Stubby seemed interested and asked a lot of questions.

I'm always amazed at how You keep putting people in our path who need to hear about You.

We still have a long way to go on this trip. Stay with us the rest of the way, Lord. And keep us safe. Here's my prayer for today:

Tell me all about your faithful love come morning time,
because I trust you.
Show me the way I should go,
because I offer my life up to you.
Deliver me from my enemies, LORD,
I seek protection from you.
Teach me to do what pleases you,
because you are my God.
Guide me by your good spirit into good land.
~ Psalms 143:8-10

July 5

Dear God,

We arrived at the Black Hills Reservation on the Fourth of July. I would have thought the natives wouldn't be into that particular holiday, but as we drove through the little village toward Red Cloud's house, kids were running all over the place, shooting off fireworks and waving flags and sparklers, and many buildings were decorated with red, white and blue banners. Strange.

Beyond the village, the reservation was a patchwork of rusted trailers, one-story clapboard houses, and tiny shacks with yards full of broken-down cars, piles of junk, and barking dogs. The Rez sits on the edge of the Black Hills, just beyond the starkly beautiful rock formations of the Badlands. For someone who had never left Buffalo in her life, it was like landing on the moon. There was something otherworldly about this land—the unexpected color, the strange rock formations that seemed to shoot up from the earth like fangs, the sudden blue of a lake, the mysterious, impenetrable darkness of the mountains... I kept thinking about the psalms that speak of the wonder of Your creation. Now I get what they are talking about.

You establish the mountains by your strength;
you are dressed in raw power.
You make the gateways of morning and evening sing for joy.
You visit the earth and make it abundant,
enriching it greatly by God's stream, full of water.
You provide people with grain because that is what you've decided.
Drenching the earth's furrows, leveling its ridges,
you soften it with rain showers; you bless its growth.
~ Psalms 65:6-10

It took us a while to find Red Cloud's house because none of the homes here have numbers. He'd described it as a brown trailer with a red pickup truck, a white van, and three old motorcycles in the front yard, none of which looked operational. As we drove up, four little kids and a teenage boy burst from the trailer to greet us. Red Cloud was a lot younger than I expected, probably seventeen. Red Cloud was only his radio call sign—his real name was Matthew. Turns out those kids were his brothers. I gave them Hershey bars, which delighted them.

Matthew invited us into the trailer, which smelled of old diapers and cigarette smoke. The smoke came from a woman sitting in a lounge chair watching television—Matthew's mom. She wore a tattered yellow t-shirt and shorts that exposed skinny legs, and ratty pink slippers on her feet. Her face had a gray pallor, and when we said hello, her eyes flicked to us without expression before returning to the TV.

Matthew gave us glasses of water from the sink. Mason and Stubby both drank, but I looked at the murky, brownish liquid and politely declined. The kids tore into their candy and soon had chocolate smeared all over their faces—one of the boys was naked except for a diaper so saturated it hung almost to his ankles.

Matthew said he would take us to meet the chief. We were about to leave when a squat old lady wearing a pink tracksuit showed up brandishing a large pot. She said she heard some radio friends of Matthew's had come for a visit, so she made her famous succotash, which she insisted we eat. Her name was Ruby. She told us, over bowlfuls of succotash which was pretty good, that she considered herself the mayor of the Rez, since she was practically the oldest resident—"they die so *young* here"—and she knew everyone's business. She was a believer and had Bible study meetings with teenagers every week at her house, Matthew included.

These kids here, she said, they want to know about Jesus. But their ancestors believed in the White Buffalo Woman, and their parents didn't believe in anything. So, they go to Ruby's for Bible study, and then they go to the Sun Dances and pray to the Great Spirit, and "they just get *confused*."

We finally got up leave, Ruby and the little boys parading with us to the car. Ruby told us to come back soon and the boys told us to bring more candy. I promised I would.

As we drove down the dirt road, I saw a teenage boy, probably Matthew's age, lying on a porch, either passed out or sleeping. Flies buzzed all around his face. That's Leonard, Matthew said. He's a friend of mine.

Matthew said he was the only one in his family with a job. He didn't know where his dad was, "maybe in prison," and his mom was too sick to work. She got a welfare check, but she still expected Matthew to hand over his paycheck every month. Matthew didn't mind—he wanted to make sure his brothers could eat.

Matthew and I were scrunched in the back seat of the Mini as we drove to the chief's house. The chief lived in a small ranch house at the end of another long dirt road. The house was painted a smoky gray color, or maybe the siding was just really dirty. As soon as we started climbing the steps to the front door, I felt that familiar coldness, the heaviness pressing against me. I knew then what the grayness covering the house was.

Matthew knocked on the door. A woman wearing a brightly colored shawl answered. She had long hair and virtually no teeth. Her neck was covered with tattoos. I took an involuntary step backward—I think it was the smell that came from her. What was that? Incense? Something really weird. Matthew introduced us and asked to see the chief.

She ushered us inside, but I held back, shaking my head. I couldn't go inside that house. I literally couldn't. My feet wouldn't move. I laughed it off and said I wasn't feeling very well, and could I stay on the porch? The woman gave me a hard look, like she knew why I wouldn't enter her house. Then she shrugged and shut the door. Matthew and Stubby looked at me strangely. I couldn't explain it to them. Mason got it, though. He knew how to read me.

A few minutes later, the door opened again, and Chief Dan Iron Eyes came out to the porch. One of his eyes was whitish and blank—I guess that was why he had that name. He looked to be around sixty, with silver hair corralled into a single, thick braid and several missing teeth. He greeted us without smiling and invited us to sit on the plastic chairs.

Matthew did most of the talking, introducing us and thanking him for allowing us to come to the reservation. Chief Iron Eyes nodded and repeated the council's demands about the radio station. Mason handed over a gold bar, which the chief took without comment.

Just then, the woman reappeared with cups of water. That smell again—I had to hold my breath as she put the tray of paper cups down on a little folding table. Chief Dan introduced the woman as Wanda Black Elk, great-granddaughter of a famous Lakota chieftain and one of the tribe's medicine women. Wanda inclined her head in greeting to the men, but to me, she leveled a glare that made the hair at the back of my neck stand up. After she went back into the house, I picked up the cup and drank the water, instantly regretting it. The water tasted warm and gritty.

Matthew suggested we ride over to the radio station, and I was the first to jump to my feet. We said goodbye to the chief and got back into the car. It was another mile to the station, a double-wide trailer shack sitting on a little rise with a twisted antenna half falling off the roof. Old equipment and stacks of record albums filled almost every nook and cranny inside.

Stubby investigated the place while making half-hearted noises of disapproval at the state of disrepair. In the end, he said he could probably salvage some of the equipment and get the station running again. We would provide the funding and even hire a couple of residents to help run it. Matthew said Chief Iron Eyes would be pleased to hear that.

Then we drove to the church, where Matthew said a mission group came to run summer camps for the Rez kids until the virus hit. The interior smelled damp and was full of black mold. There was graffiti all over the walls—it was in Lakota, so I couldn't read it, but I imagined it was not too complimentary. A skeleton had been hung upon the large cross over the alter. All the windows were smashed. I felt that coldness again, that sense of being suffocated—this place needed an exorcism badly.

We talked about what we needed to do to get the church livable, and I suggested we stay for the summer. We could live in tents and work on the church. The others agreed.

I'm actually pretty excited about this. I mean, it will be a lot of work, but it feels like, for once, we can actually *do* something. That this is a battle we can fight and win. Who knows? Maybe we can actually make this church a real church one day. We can invite people to come and hear about You. We can do something good for these people, I hope, and they can help us too.

I just want to say thanks. For getting us here safely. For what You are going to do next.

Give thanks to the one who made the skies with skill—
God's faithful love lasts forever.
Give thanks to the one who shaped the earth on the water—
God's faithful love lasts forever.
Give thanks to the one who made the great lights—
God's faithful love lasts forever.
Give thanks to the God of heaven—
God's faithful love lasts forever!
~ Psalms 136:5-7,26

YEAR TEN

Resistance

YBR via Shortwave #93

Greetings from Munchkin land! We are definitely not in Kansas anymore.

Many of you have asked how we're doing. It's been quite a ride, to be sure. A brave, new, mad, mad world. We are reminded every day that no matter what is happening around us, God is still in control.

We've heard from many of you, all over the world. God makes a way! The Ozzies aren't listening in, as far as we know. Or maybe they just don't care. Either way, we will keep bringing you what news we gather and remind you of the truth—that no matter how bleak it gets, we know who wins. Our job is to endure.

First, the news: Zazel has made good on his promise to end the war—the Alliance is currently in peace talks with Israel. Alliance nations were looking for an excuse to stop shooting anyway, since they were almost out of bullets. The world rejoices at being at peace because it does not yet know what that peace will cost.

Zazel has made another conquest as well: Shannon Snow. Harry Ravel resigned as President of the United States in order to work directly for Zazel as his personal spiritual counselor—or something. That might have shocked the world, but it didn't shock us. Ravel knows where the real power is. Besides, we are fairly sure Mrs. Ravel insisted. This means she will spend quite a bit of time in New Asgard. She has made no bones of her admiration for the Supreme Leader and has probably had more photo ops with him than anyone else in the world, including Ravel himself.

Ravel's successor, Vice President Devon Newman, has promised to continue the work Ravel started. To combat the climate crisis, he has passed more laws restricting energy usage, fertilizers, meat and dairy production, large-scale farming, and gas-powered vehicles. He's shut down the pipelines and put a moratorium on oil exploration and drilling. This means, of course, that if you weren't starving before, you will be now.

Natural disasters are on the upswing: a seven hundred percent uptick in earthquakes, a four hundred percent increase in hurricanes and monsoons, and a *fourteen hundred percent* rise in volcanic activity, which has created a black cloud over almost all northern Europe as well as the Pacific Rim. A meteor about 300 feet wide hit the Russian city of Perm last week, killing over ten thousand and virtually wiping out the city as well as much of the Ural Mountains. A meteor that size has the strength of ten nuclear bombs.

Is all this because of the climate crisis—or are we under the judgment of God?

What do you think? Read Revelation 6. Get your hearts right with God. Prepare for the fight of your life.

January 7

Dear God,

An earthquake hit Buffalo, demolishing most of downtown. The city hall is a toppling ruin. Four apartment buildings collapsed. Many people are dead. We felt the tremor in the Hole. We never get earthquakes here. It's happening more and more. Everywhere.

It's so cold we have to wear several layers of clothing, even in the Hobbit Hole. Not enough fuel for heat. Barely enough to cook with. Ralph wears two scarves around his neck. He's been coughing a lot, too.

We're getting ready to head back to the Black Hills. Stubby's last message was encouraging—he and Matthew and some of the Lakota kids are still working on the church, which took longer than we had hoped to fix up with materials in short supply. At least most of the mold is gone, and the roof is whole again.

Stubby's got the radio station up and running too, and on clear nights we can pick up his signal with our short wave. I can't wait to go back—not only to see Matthew and Ruby and the other friends we've made on the Rez but also to get out of the Hobbit Hole and Buffalo, which has become more like a prison. Just going outside is dangerous.

Ralph has retreated more and more into himself, studying his prophecy books by candlelight. Miss Em and Ripley huddle in the Lair, working on the YBR radio shows.

Last week, Mason and I found two boys nearly frozen to death hiding out in a junkyard—we'd gone there to find radio parts for

Ripley. We brought them to the Hole, where Miss Em fed them, and they told us their story.

Jackson is thirteen, Josh eleven. Their parents were Re-FUS-ERs, though their dad, Jerry, scratched out a living by doing odd jobs for their neighbors. One day, he got a pain in his chest, and he thought he was having a heart attack. His wife got scared and took him to the hospital. The hospital sent him to the quarantine camp. Turns out Jerry wasn't having a heart attack, just angina pain, but they wouldn't release him. Instead, the Peacemakers went to their house, got their sons, and brought them to the camp.

The camp doctor refused to release them until they got FUSED. Jerry wouldn't do it. He'd worked for a newspaper before being fired, and he knew the media was suppressing information about the Cure. The doctor said he was going to FUSE the boys anyway, without his consent. There was a new law that said parental consent was no longer required for any medical procedure.

So, Jerry helped his sons escape by climbing over the fence during the night. He had told them to go to a friend's house, but the boys had gotten lost and chased by Peacemakers, and they'd ended up in the junkyard. They'd been there for five days with no food.

I can't imagine what those parents are going through, not knowing what happened to their kids. We're going to get a message to them, maybe even get them released. Desmond is working on that.

Thank You for leading us to these kids. Thank You for saving them. Please protect Jerry and his wife. Help us get them out of there.

> *"Be still, and know that I am God.*
> *I will be exalted among the nations,*
> *I will be exalted in the earth!"*
> *The Lord of hosts is with us;*
> *the God of Jacob is our fortress.*
> *~ Psalms 46:10-11*

January 18

Dear God,

Prayer request: we need new transportation to go to South Dakota. We have too many people to fit in the Mini, and the Psycho-Van won't make it all the way, Mason thinks. Besides Jackson and Josh, who are still sleeping on the floor in the Hole, we now have a young couple named Sam and Jenny who wanted to get married but were told they weren't allowed to because they didn't have enough crypto credits. That's a thing now. A social credit system that rates you for everything you do. You need a certain number of credits in order to get married, have children, own a home, a car, buy meat, almost anything. The credits are earned through good behavior, though the rules for that keep changing. I guess they don't want ordinary people to do those things anymore.

Jenny was told she should sign up to be a birth mother for the Grigori. The Grigori have started a new program to repopulate the world with their own offspring—kind of like what the Watchers did the first time around. A woman at the implanting center told Jenny that if she had a couple of Grigori babies, she would earn enough crypto to get a marriage license. Many of Jenny's friends had already signed up for the "We Birth" program. But Jenny was appalled.

Sam explained that they had always been Get-the-Cure-Follow-the-Rules types because they believed the government had their best interests at heart. But this was too far. They cut out their own chips and came to us.

I feel a little like I'm drowning today. Too much bad news. Too many problems. If we somehow got a bigger vehicle, how are we going to get the gas? How will we feed all these people? Where will we put them when we get to the Rez? Is there any hope that we are going to make it through?

I know this psalm was written for Israel, but I'm claiming it for myself. For Penny.

LORD, my heart isn't proud;
my eyes aren't conceited.
I don't get involved with things
too great or wonderful for me. No.

But I have calmed and quieted myself
like a weaned child on its mother;
I'm like the weaned child that is with me.
Penny, wait for the LORD — from now until forever from now!
~ Psalms 131:1-3

February 1

Dear God,

I'm pregnant.

I don't know whether to be happy or scared out of my mind. I think I'm both.

I felt really sick on the drive to the Rez. I thought it was just riding in the back of the van that made me sick, with the smell of the gas cans and all those people crammed together and all, and Mason took a lot of rutted back roads to avoid drones. Thank You for the new van, by the way! I think I forgot to say that before. One of our new passengers had it hidden in his garage. You always provide.

I happened to mention to Ruby that I was nauseous all the time, and she knew exactly what was happening. So, I picked up a test at the pharmacy in Rapid City, and sure enough, it was positive.

A baby.

I thought Mason would be upset—he was thrilled. He didn't think he could have kids, given what he'd done to his body with drugs through the years. I assumed the same thing. So maybe this is a miracle.

I'm still scared, but in a weird way, this gives me hope. Life finds a way. I finally understand the truth of this psalm.

You are the one who created my innermost parts;
you knit me together while I was still in my mother's womb.
I give thanks to you that I was marvelously set apart.
Your works are wonderful—I know that very well.
My bones weren't hidden from you
when I was being put together in a secret place,
when I was being woven together

in the deep parts of the earth.
Your eyes saw my embryo,
and on your scroll every day
was written that was being formed for me,
before any one of them had yet happened.
~ Psalms 139:13-16

Meanwhile, we have so much work to do here. The church is coming along, but we need more space if we are going to keep bringing people to the Rez. The tribal council has given us another condemned building to use for housing, and so we're hiring more workers and scrounging through second-hand shops in Rapid City and Custer for supplies. Thankfully, here in South Dakota, you can still buy things with cash in most stores. A few more of the natives have stepped up to help us—we pay them in gold and Hershey bars. I'm trying to be helpful, but it's tough with the morning sickness, which seems to last all day. I'm so tired too—I just want to sleep. Mason patched up the best air mattress he could find and told me to take it easy, but it's hard when everyone around you is working and, well, there's so much work to do.

The two kids, Jackson and Josh, are doing okay. I promised them we would help their parents—it's the only reason they agreed to come to the Rez. Please help Desmond get their parents out.

Ruby threw a big party to celebrate my pregnancy. She made a gigantic pot of her succotash and invited all the neighbors. Even Matthew's mom came, looking almost clear-eyed. It was pretty cold, but the guys built a big fire in Ruby's fire pit, and Mason provided hot dogs on sticks for everyone to roast themselves. We met a lot of nice people, though many seemed wary of us. Chief Dan and Wanda came too. Wanda wore a head-to-toe outfit made of bleached white buffalo hide, just like the White Buffalo Woman. The spiritual scent on her was still very strong—I kept far away from her, even though I felt her wintry gaze on me from across the yard. Maybe she senses Your Spirit on me, the way I sense those dark spirits on her.

Lord, protect us from whatever spirits are lurking here in this place. Send your angels to surround us and keep us safe.

For he will command his angels concerning you

to guard you in all your ways.
On their hands they will bear you up,
lest you strike your foot against a stone.
~ Psalms 91:11-12

May 10

Dear God,

He's gone now. He was here for so short a time. I never felt him move—him or her. I never knew that either.

A few days after we got home from the Rez, I woke up with terrible cramps. Blood on the bed. I knew what was happening. Did You hear my prayers? Did You just ignore them? Or did You answer, and Your answer was no?

I wish I had more faith.

Miss Em helped me. She said it happens a lot with first-time pregnancies. She seems to know about these things. It wasn't my fault. There will be others. I know she was trying to make me feel better.

I haven't moved a muscle in two days—my whole body aches. My heart aches. My soul aches. Everything.

I know I shouldn't blame You. But I can't help but ask—why did You let this happen? I can accept many things. Struggles and pain and hard times. But for some things, like this, I just want a reason. I want to know that there *is* a reason. That it matters.

What did he look like? He or she. Would he have dark hair, like Mason, and brown eyes, like me? Would he be short or tall? Would he have been smart? Liked music or art or books? We would have taught him to love You as soon as he was born.

Then again, maybe no one should be born into the world the way it's going.

Mason seems to be over it. Either that, or he's trying to be strong for me. Whenever I talk about the baby, he changes the subject and talks about all the new plans for the Rez or the new Re-FUSERS we need to rescue. I only half listen. I really don't even care right now.

Miss Em brings me tea and soup and tells me I need to eat. I can't keep anything down. This morning she sat on my bed and prayed with me like she used to when I was first getting clean. Her prayers felt like a…a parachute. Does that sound strange? Having this happen was like being shoved off a cliff. But Miss Em's prayers were like a parachute opening over me, so I would fall more slowly. Gently.

This is what she quoted. I'm just going to repeat this one over and over until it sticks.

My flesh and my heart may fail,
but God is the strength of my heart and my portion forever.
~ Psalms 73:26

August 12

Dear God,

It's been three months, but I still feel the emptiness. I thought I'd be over it by now. Maybe I'll never be over it until it happens again. And yet I don't feel ready to pray for another baby. Not now. Not in this world. Not until we're in a better place.

I still wake up every morning stabbed by guilt—that it happened because I wasn't good enough to be a mother. I've made too many mistakes, screwed up my body. Help me stop thinking those things. Paul says we need to "take captive every thought," and I'm trying. But those thoughts keep escaping and attacking me again.

Mason is getting mad because I won't let him touch me. I just…can't. We've always been able to find solace in each other, but now I push him away. I don't want to. I just can't help it. Isn't that something Paul said too? Why do I do the things I don't want to do? Something like that. I feel you, Paul.

I don't know why I worry so much about myself and my own problems when there are so many bigger problems. Like civil war. The governors of Montana, Alaska, Wyoming, North and South Dakota, and Nebraska have refused to follow the new federal mandates. The president had a meltdown on TV and cut off all funding to the Re-FUSER states—he even instituted an official travel ban to any state that won't comply. Now there is open talk about a formal secession. It's the same in some of the southern states: Texas, Oklahoma, Arkansas, Mississippi, Louisiana, Alabama, and Florida. Thirteen altogether. People are calling us the Divided States of America now.

Some good news: Desmond got Jackson and Josh's parents released from the camp! They are planning to go to South Dakota on our next trip. Just in time, too—I'm worried that it might soon be a lot tougher to travel.

Thank you, Lord, for sustaining us, even when we don't know where our next meal is coming from.

You prepare a table before me
in the presence of my enemies.
You anoint my head with oil;
my cup overflows.
~ Psalms 23:5

August 28

Dear God,

Blaine was arrested again. This time it's worse than ever. He might never get out.

He had reopened his church in a new location, an abandoned warehouse in Black Rock. Mason helped put up flyers all over the city. I didn't think it was such a good idea, given what's happened before, but Blaine said he felt God calling him to reach out to the people of the city who needed to hear Your word.

I was kind of surprised to hear that the city was allowing church services to resume, but it's only under certain conditions. All attendees have to be FUSED, and the preacher cannot say anything that goes against the new speech guidelines set down by the government. To me, it seemed like a trap. But Blaine was determined.

Mason and I went to the first service, even though we weren't FUSED. I doubted most of the people there had been. About fifty attended, sitting on crates and lawn chairs, whatever Blaine could find. Several wore scarves and face masks, even though it was wickedly hot in that place. Probably to hide their identities more than fear of the virus.

Blaine's friend Joe played the guitar, and we sang some songs, our voices magnified by the high ceilings. We prayed, and then Blaine started preaching. Mason recorded the whole thing on an old camcorder Ripley gave him, so I could write down the sermon and remember it forever.

"My friends. Listen to these words of Paul: 'It is for freedom that Christ set you free.' Galatians 5:1.

"What does freedom mean? The freedom to do whatever you want without consequences? Nope. The freedom Paul spoke of is not freedom *to*, but freedom *from*. Freedom from sin. Freedom from slavery. Freedom from oppressive rules that wear you down and make you a slave to *this* world. Paul was speaking specifically to those who wanted the Gentiles to submit to the Law of Moses to be saved. All that was needed, Paul said, was faith in Jesus Christ. He had an uphill battle getting the Jerusalem Council to hear and heed his message, but in the end, he won that argument.

"Today, we are fighting a similar battle. The world tells us that in order to be saved, we must submit to an experimental medical procedure with no precedent, the long-term effects of which are still unknown. We must also have a chip implanted in our bodies to track our activity and behavior and ensure we get regular infusions. Those who don't do these things are a danger to society and therefore excluded from participating in any public activity, including church, school, shopping, or walking in the park.

"Even church leaders have signed on to this mandate, citing Romans 13, where Paul told believers to submit to authority. This is what Romans 13 says:

Let every person be subject to the governing authorities.
For there is no authority except from God,
and those that exist have been instituted by God.
Therefore, whoever resists the authorities resists what God has appointed,
and those who resist will incur judgment.
~ Romans 13:1-2

"Does this mean we must submit to the current authority in every way at all times? It would seem so.

"But let me ask you this question. Did Daniel submit to authority when he refused to worship the king? Did Shadrach, Me-shach, and Abednego submit to authority when they refused to bow down to a statue? Did the Israelites in Egypt submit to authority when they resisted Pharaoh? Did Jesus submit to authority when he called the Sanhedrin snakes and the Pharisees white-washed tombs? Did John the Baptist submit to authority when he rebuked Herod for marrying his brother's wife? Did the disciples submit to authority when they refused to heed the orders of the Sanhedrin not to speak about Jesus? Did Paul himself submit to authority when he escaped arrest by being lowered from a basket outside the wall?

"You see, submission to authority is generally a good thing. God is a God of order, not chaos. Without authority, there would be anarchy. But along with that, there is room for holy disobedience. When man's laws oppose God's laws, the Christ-follower must choose God's law over man's authority.

"Let me put it this way: would you, if you lived in Nazi Germany, submit to a law that told you to put Jews in concentration camps? What if an SS soldier commanded you to turn in your friends and neighbors? If you were a doctor, and the governor of this state told you not to treat a Re-FUSER—would you do it?

"Some people do. Many people do. Few people, in this present darkness, resist.

"In the last several years, we've witnessed many remarkable events. We've seen people censored, ostracized from society, and even thrown into prison camps because they refused to submit to authority. Our rulers say we can no longer eat meat or drive cars because it is bad for the environment. You notice, of course, that these rulers continue to fly around the world in their private jets and sail in luxury yachts. They buy houses by the sea and eat sumptuous meals, all while telling you, *you* must sacrifice and endure more pain and privation for the common good. They will eat steak, but you will eat crickets. Is this lawful? Is it moral?

"They have also told us we can no longer preach from any part of the Holy Bible that, according to them, foments hatred and bigotry. There is a new bible now—I happen to have a copy of it."

At this point, Blaine held up the *new* bible, which looked to be about a quarter the size of a real Bible. People in the audience leaned in—most of us never even knew there was a new bible that all religious leaders were told they must use.

"This is the government-approved Bible. Do you know what is missing? All the passages to do with slaves, of course, including most of Exodus and Leviticus. Passages that refer to all life as sacred are gone, including the unborn. Adam and Eve are missing, too, for we may not know that God created man and woman. Anything to do with marriage is also gone, for we can no longer preach that God created marriage between a man and a woman and that there is such a thing as sexual immorality. In fact, sin itself has been stricken from this book, except for the sin of disobeying the ruling authorities.

Is this right? Is it moral? Should we submit to this overreaching power? Or should we resist? Should we stand up and say, 'No!'"

Someone from the audience jumped to their feet, fist in the air, shouting, "No!" Others soon joined in, clapping and shouting, "Resist!" and "God's rules, not man's rules!" and other such things. Suddenly, this solemn little gathering of fearful people had turned into a holy mob.

That's when the door burst open, and the room flooded with Peacemakers. They stormed up to the platform, seized Blaine, and threw him to the floor. People ran every which way as more Peacemakers burst in, grabbing and scanning people. Mason took my hand and dragged me away from the chaos—we escaped through another door on the side of the building and ran back to the Hobbit Hole. I felt guilty for leaving Blaine and the others, but there was nothing we could do for them. Blaine must have known what would happen. He *wanted* it to happen. Like Paul, he got himself arrested so he could make his case before judges and rulers.

The story came out in the paper the next morning—I went to the train station to get a copy.

Blaine Humphries, thirty-three, was arrested during an illegal church service yesterday afternoon. Preliminary charges involve fomenting hate speech, unlawful assembly, and disturbing the peace. He is being held under guard at the East Side Quarantine Camp pending further investigation. Mr. Humphries has been previously incarcerated for inciting riots and disturbing the peace. This arrest marks his third in the "three strikes law" and means that, if convicted, Mr. Humphries faces a maximum penalty of life in prison.

Not a single church leader has come to Blaine's defense.

Ralph called Desmond, who thought Blaine's prospects were dim. With his prior convictions, he was most likely already condemned. The government will want to make an example of him.

More words from Psalm 91. I think you are talking to Blaine here. He needs Your protection and Your peace.

Because he holds fast to me in love,
I will deliver him; I will protect him,
because he knows my name.
When he calls to me, I will answer him;
I will be with him in trouble;
I will rescue him and honor him.
With long life I will satisfy him and show him my salvation.
~ Psalms 91:14-16

September 2

Dear God,

I just woke up from a terrible dream. I didn't want to wake Mason, so I'm telling You instead. It was about Blaine. I dreamt he went to the guillotine—like it was the French Revolution.

I think the dream was a warning. From you. They are going to do something terrible to him. Make an example of him. So that anyone who speaks in Your name will be silenced for good.

We need to get him out of there. Lord, you've helped your followers in prison before. You helped Mason and Jerry and his wife. I beg you…please do it again. Get Blaine out of the camp. Soon! Send angels. Send me.

Whenever I need a word from You, I open my Bible and read the first verse I see.

This is the word You gave me this morning:

Make your ways known to me, LORD;
teach me your paths.
Lead me in your truth—teach it to me—
because you are the God who saves me.

I put my hope in you all day long.
~ Psalms 25:4-5

September 14

Dear God,

Trial date is set for April 12. Desmond's motions to dismiss have been denied.

Mason's talked me into going back to the Rez with him. He says I need a distraction. We will reunite Jackson and Josh with their parents—they are anxious to leave.

I don't know if I can make another trip out there. I feel so...depleted. I just want to give up. Quit everything. Sleep forever.

Lord, help me have hope again. I need a reminder of why I must keep fighting.

I usually skip this psalm because it's so long. But this time, I read it all the way through. Especially this part. It's like I could have written this myself.

My whole being yearns for your saving help!
I wait for your promise. My eyes are worn out looking for your
word.
"When will you comfort me?"
I ask, because I've become like a bottle dried up by smoke,
though I haven't forgotten your statutes.
How much more time does your servant have?
When will you bring my oppressors to justice?
The arrogant have dug pits for me—
those people who act against your Instruction.
All your commandments are true, but people harass me for no reason.
Help me! They've almost wiped me off the face of the earth!
Meanwhile, I haven't abandoned your precepts!
Make me live again according to your faithful love
so I can keep the law you've given!
~ Psalms 119:81-88

December 14

Dear God,

I'm thirty years old today. At least I think this is my birthday. I've never actually known for sure.

I never thought I'd live to see twenty, let alone thirty. I'm only here because of You.

I feel old. More like a hundred. My bones ache. My stomach growls all day long. My hair has been falling out. Miss Em says it's stress. She gave me a brand-new bottle of purple hair dye for my birthday. I don't even know where she got it. Miss Em has secret superpowers.

Mason gave me a leather bracelet he made himself, with the help of one of Matthew's friends who's good with leather crafts. Miss Em made a cake, and she even had ice cream. No idea where she got it—like I said, she's got superpowers. I ate like a fiend. Later that night, I crawled in beside Mason, and we held each other for a long time. It felt good to be with him again and not be afraid. He told me to remember that whatever happened, You were in control. He believes that because he's lived it. I have to. I should know to just trust You. Why do I have to keep learning the same lesson over and over? Sometimes I can be so dense.

This morning I opened my Bible, and this psalm jumped out at me. It was perfect. Gratitude.

> *Bless the Lord , O my soul,*
> *and all that is within me, bless his holy name!*
> *Bless the Lord , O my soul,*
> *and forget not all his benefits,*
> *who forgives all your iniquity,*
> *who heals all your diseases,*
> *who redeems your life from the pit,*
> *who crowns you with steadfast love and mercy,*
> *who satisfies you with good*
> *so that your youth is renewed like the eagle's.*
> *~ Psalms 103:1-5*

YEAR ELEVEN

The Forbidden

YBR via Shortwave #100

Greetings, Munchkins. Auntie Em here. I know it has been a while. We've had technical difficulties—lots of them. Since we can't tell you when we will broadcast in advance, we will repeat this message several times over the next few days hoping everyone hears it.

First, the latest news from the Guild.

We knew it was coming, but now it has happened. Grigori Zazel dissolved the United Nations and formed a new ruling world government, the United Earth. All 195 countries of the world are now divided into ten regions: The North American Union, the South American Union, the African Union, the Middle East Union, the Russian Union, the Chinasian Union, the Scandinavian Union, the European Union, the Indian Union, and the South Pacific Union. Each Union is headed by a Leader forming the Council of Ten, who will distribute the world's resources equally and equitably among the Unions. The new council has declared this a wonderful new era of Global Peace and Prosperity for all.

There has been little opposition to this plan. Most nations were already broken by years of pandemics, Rages, natural disasters, economic stagnation, famine, severe energy shortages, and societal breakdown. While some may not want Grigori Zazel as their overlord, they fear him as their adversary.

The new world government has a name for those who oppose their agenda: The Forbidden. Those who still refuse to get the Cure and the chip are now forbidden from participating in the public sphere. What has been happening piecemeal for years is now codified into global law.

Only thirteen of the former United States continue to resist joining a union and have formed two independent territories—the Northern Free States and the Southern Free States. Interestingly, Supreme Lord Grigori Zazel has told the NAU not to oppose the states' secession. Most likely, he believes the Free States, which he refers to as the Forbidden States, will soon run out of resources and surrender on their own. He's probably not wrong—the alliance of the Free States is a tenuous thing, with several militia leaders vying for supremacy.

It should be noted that Israel has refused, so far, to join a union.

It's an open question whether Chinasia is going to stick with the UE in the long term. It doesn't need Zazel or the UE—it owns almost all the technology required for the advanced Grigori machines and weaponry, as well as most of the world's lithium, cobalt, nickel, copper, graphite, manganese, and aluminum mines. Zazel must have promised the Chinasian leader the moon and the stars to get him to join.

In a few weeks, the Council of Ten will meet for the first time—the meeting will be broadcast on TV screens and the brand new HOLOs, hologram viewers, across the world. If you no longer have a television or a HOLO, keep listening to this station for updates.

Closer to home, we ask for your prayers for our brother, Pastor Blaine, who's still held in a quarantine camp, awaiting trial. We can get little information about his condition, only that he's alive and preparing his defense. He knows you are praying for him, and those prayers will sustain him.

We will do everything we can to help you get to a Free State, should you need it. Since South Dakota has seceded, we no longer need to confine ourselves to just the Black Hills reservation for a safe zone, although we will continue to do so if the NAU changes its mind about invading. Several other reservations have opened enrollment to non-Indians who seek asylum as well, although all must agree to follow tribal laws.

God bless you, dear friends. Remember how much He loves you.

February 2

Dear God,

Ralph and Miss Em are getting so skinny. Even Ripley looks thin, which is kind of amazing. He calls it the Forbidden diet. We're eating plain pasta, canned foods, peanut butter, and crackers. Miss Em still makes her hot chocolate without whipped cream and marshmallows. On our next trip to SD, we'll have to get some food and supplies to bring back to the Hobbit Hole.

The stores that would take cash are gone now—closed up. We used to have some chipped people who would sell us their rations for twice the price, but they won't anymore. Too scared of getting caught and sent to a camp. Besides, they barely have enough for themselves.

I keep telling Ralph it's time to leave. We should move to SD before it's too late. He still refuses. You know what I think? I think he's still waiting for Jared and Grace to come home. If we leave, they won't know how to find us. I know that's what he's thinking. I even asked Miss Em about it. She just shook her head and started to cry.

We just learned that President Newman, now the leader of the NAU, has launched more drones over the Forbidden states to catch people attempting to cross the border. Mason says we need to find alternative routes to avoid getting caught. He's not even sure it's possible.

Nothing is impossible with You. If You want us to go, You'll make a way. That is why David wrote this psalm—my prayer for today.

> *The Lord is my shepherd, I lack nothing.*
> *He makes me lie down in green pastures,*
> *he leads me beside quiet waters,*
> *he refreshes my soul.*
> *He guides me along the right paths for his name's sake.*
> *Even though I walk through the darkest valley,*
> *I will fear no evil, for you are with me;*
> *your rod and your staff, they comfort me.*
> *You prepare a table before me in the presence of my enemies.*
> *You anoint my head with oil; my cup overflows.*
> *Surely your goodness and love will follow me all the days of my life,*
> *and I will dwell in the house of the Lord forever.'*
> *~ Psalms 23*

February 28

Dear God,

It's nice being back in the Black Hills. We made it, thanks to

You. It snowed most of the way, which slowed us down but also helped hide us from the drones.

I was so thrilled to see Jackson and Josh reunited with their parents. We bought a house for them in a fairly new neighborhood, where the government had rebuilt the homes after a major flood fifteen years ago. Sam and Jenny are also going to live there. The one-story bungalow needed work, but we put in new carpeting and painted the exterior a sunny yellow. The other refugees are living either at the church or in a couple of trailers we acquired with a few bars of gold to the tribal council. Some are still living in tents until we get places for them.

Speaking of the tribal council, we met with them this morning. They are getting ornery about all the people we're bringing to the Rez, even though we keep handing over the gold. I'm pretty sure the council members are hoarding it—the natives aren't getting any of that. But what can we do? The council is in charge. I saw that Chief Dan Iron Eyes got all new siding on his house and a brand-new pickup truck. I guess he's doing okay from the money we're giving the tribe.

The radio station is on the air twelve hours a day, thanks to Stubby and his new recruits. The network is growing quickly— more people who have lost internet access are on shortwave.

One of the people that contacted us is Kent Roland, a Montana rancher who got into a shootout with the Ozzies when they tried to take over his cattle ranch. He's organized a militia, and people from all over the Free states are flocking to him, including the National Guardsmen and military personnel kicked out because they wouldn't take the Cure. Anyway, Roland wants to meet with us. We're going to drive to Montana in a couple of days.

I just want to thank You for this safe haven. I pray you will continue to protect us—protect all the people here who have put their trust in You alone.

I read this psalm today—I love David's passion! Don't You?

Let all who want to kill me
be disgraced and put to shame.
Chase away and confuse all
who plan to harm me.
Send your angel after them
and let them be like straw in the wind.

Make them run in the dark on a slippery road,
as your angel chases them.
~ Psalms 35:4-6

March 3

Dear God,

Roland is quite a character. Tall and reedy, swears a blue streak and spits tobacco right on the floor. He's a big fan of the YBR and thinks we should join forces.

I told him all about what we were doing on the Rez and asked what steps we could take to protect ourselves in the event of an invasion. He told me that with the size of the Rez and the natives being so spread out and not being well-armed, our best chance was to hide. The Black Hills themselves were a great hiding place—almost everyone on the Great Plains would head our way in the event of an invasion, including him. Who knew what sort of invasion it would be anyway—tanks? Bombs? Nuclear weapons? With the Grigori in play, it might be something no one has ever seen before. There wasn't a lot we could do about that. But Roland figured they would try starving us out first, an old-fashioned siege. The Ozzies, he used that nickname—something we coined—don't expect us to hold out for long. Maybe a couple of years at the most. They aren't in that big of a hurry. We have to be smarter, he said. And we have to be united, despite being spread out all over the place. That was going to be the hardest part. Re-FUSERS are not joiners by nature, so it might be like herding cats.

Before we left, I asked him if he believed in Jesus. He just shrugged and said he hadn't thought about it much. He was too busy trying to save his ranch. I told him if he ever wanted to talk about it, he should let me know. He said he would, although he didn't sound too interested. But you never know.

Lord, take care of Roland. He's taken on a lot. He's not that young, and he doesn't know you, but he's doing your work anyway.

We'll head home in a few days, back to Buffalo—Blaine's trial is starting soon. I dread going back. I dread the long drive through what is now enemy territory, worried we might run out of gas or have a breakdown, get caught by drones or Peacemakers in their new flying cars—I dread the darkness and depression of the Hobbit Hole, the constant fear of getting arrested for something I didn't even know was illegal.

Not that I want to give up on Grace and Jared, but it's been eleven years. How long should we wait? Are they still alive by some miracle? I know nothing is impossible with You, but still…I don't want to live on false hope, either. And I'm not sure how much time we have left.

I remember this promise You made in Psalm 32 like You were talking directly to me:

I will instruct you and teach you
about the direction you should go.
I'll advise you and keep my eye on you.
~ Psalms 32:8

YBR via Shortwave #101

Greetings Munchkins,

We begin with sad news. Our friend Pastor Blaine has been convicted of spreading hate speech and misinformation, criticizing the government, and holding an unauthorized assembly, which has now been deemed a protest. The judge gave him twenty years, claiming he was a danger to society, and the sentence should be a warning to all the Forbidden—this is what happens when you refuse to follow the rules.

No cameras or recording devices were allowed in the courtroom while the pastor and his lawyer presented their defense, so of course, the media has distorted and censored Blaine's words for the sake of their current narrative. However, we will continue to broadcast Blaine's final sermon every day, so you will know the truth of what happened and what he actually said.

The judge also ordered Pastor Blaine be moved from the quarantine camp in Buffalo to a maximum-security camp built exclusively for the Forbidden in the northern part of the NAU, probably the Yukon, old Canada's version of Siberia.

This is not the outcome we had hoped for, but it was not unexpected. They would put all the Forbidden in camps if they could. The media hailed the decision as a triumph for freedom and democracy—I'm not kidding. They actually said so. We are all safer, they say, with people like Pastor Blaine off the streets. The same does not go for actual criminals, of course, who have been given free rein to loot and pillage to their hearts' content.

Meanwhile, the Ozzies are figuring out new ways to track those of us who are not FUSED or chipped. They have drones, of course, but drones can be avoided, and we've gotten pretty good at that. However, the Grigori have introduced new technologies like Smart Dust—tiny nanoparticles released into the atmosphere to monitor human activity and send information back to a central host. And Smart Water, nanotech particles added to the water supply. Even the Forbidden drink water, right? The Ozzies won't need your compliance to get their Cure into you—they will simply put it in your water. Or they might use mosquitoes—Cure-carrying mosquitoes are also currently in trials and may be released within a year.

Does all this sound like a conspiracy theory? I ask you, how many crazy conspiracy theories have proven true in the last ten years? Is anything too absurd anymore?

April 14

Dear God,

Blaine got twenty years.

I still can't believe it.

How can this be? For preaching the Bible?

The world has gone crazy.

Last night I had that dream again about the guillotine. I woke up in a cold sweat, my heart beating so wildly I thought it would jump out of my chest. My gasping woke Mason up, and he usually sleeps through everything. We have to get him out of there, I said. Now. Before they take him to prison.

You will make a way, won't You? It's what You do, right? Like you did when your people walked through the Red Sea.

Your road led through the sea,
your pathway through the mighty waters—
a pathway no one knew was there!
~ Psalms 77:19

I read somewhere that the Red Sea was too deep for two million people to cross the lake bed with wagons and livestock in one night, but a land bridge in one spot would have been wide enough to accommodate all those people. An explorer in the 1970s discovered it when he was researching the exact place where the crossing might have happened, using details from Exodus. The explorer even found chariot wheels in that very spot.

You can make a way when there seems to be no way. I'm asking You now. DO IT AGAIN.

But I will remember the LORD's deeds;
yes, I will remember your wondrous acts from times long past.
I will meditate on all your works; I will ponder your deeds.
~ Psalms 77:11-12

April 23

Dear God,

You did it.

I have to write it down so that someday, someone will read this and know what You did for us. It was almost like the Red Sea all over again.

After my dream, the five of us spent a whole day discussing how to get Blaine out of that camp. Ralph didn't even want us to try. Too risky, he said. We'd all end up sent to a camp or, worse, the Yukon. Miss Em seemed to agree, though she didn't say much, just kept fussing with the teapot. Ripley and Mason brainstormed all kinds of ideas, like stealing an ambulance and smuggling Blaine out in a body bag. But getting in and out of the camp station without a chip was the hard part. The only way in was as a Peacemaker or a prisoner. Visitors, even if they were allowed, had to be FUSED and chipped.

That's what gave me the idea.

When I told them my plan, they all said no. But I talked them into it. I could handle it. You would take care of me. I wasn't afraid. I sounded way more sure of that than I felt.

I believe—help my unbelief!

The night before we carried it out, I memorized this psalm, a psalm of David, because I needed more courage and faith than ever before. And I will need you to hide me in a secret place—in your tent.

The LORD is my light and my salvation.
Should I fear anyone?
The LORD is a fortress protecting my life.
Should I be frightened of anything?
He will shelter me in his own dwelling during troubling times;
He will hide me in a secret place in his own tent;
He will set me up high, safe on a rock.
~ Psalms 27:1,5

We didn't sleep much the night before. We spent the next day preparing. Mason bleached his hair blond—with his pale skin, he looked like a ghost. Miss Em helped him pad his clothes to give him more bulk, and she lent him a pair of wedge heels to make him look taller. She found a red dress in her closet and altered it to fit me. We went over the plan several times, figuring what to do in case something went wrong.

When it was time to go, Miss Em prayed for us and Ralph spoke a Bible verse over us, the command You and Moses gave to Joshua before sending him to conquer the Promised Land:

Be strong and courageous. Do not be afraid, for the Lord is with
you wherever you go.

Ralph told us that You repeated that command several times—maybe because Joshua was just as scared as we are now.

As soon as it was dark, Ripley drove us in the Mini to the east end of the city, where the East Side Quarantine Camp lay. He pulled over a couple of blocks from the main entrance in front of an abandoned house, behind a rusted car with only two wheels. He said he would wait there and gave Mason a walkie-talkie to keep him updated.

Mason and I got out of the van and stood on the sidewalk, looking at each other. Then Mason pulled me into his arms, hugging me with such fierceness I couldn't breathe. He was trembling as much as I was. He told me not to be afraid—I said the same thing to him. We both laughed. I could just hear Grace's voice in my head:

When has saying don't be afraid ever made anyone not afraid?
Be strong and courageous. Do not be afraid, for the Lord is with
you wherever you go.

When You say it, maybe it works.

Finally, he let go, turned down a side street, and disappeared from view. I adjusted my dress, smoothed back my hair, and walked toward the main gate, my head high, though my stomach churned and my knees wobbled.

A gate guard watched me approach and barred my way. I've come to see a prisoner, I said. He looked me up and down—I think he wanted to turn me away but decided I was harmless and directed me toward the station, a squat, metal building set off to the side of the gate.

Inside, the station was stuffy and smelled of disinfectant. The fluorescent lighting painted the walls a sickly green, made ghastlier by huge posters of Grigori plastered everywhere. I swallowed hard and focused on the female Peacemaker behind the counter. I had never seen a female Peacemaker before. She had stark white hair cut very short and steel blue eyes that tracked me without expression as I approached. A couple of male Peacemakers were standing guard at the side doors, still as statues, their faces hidden by masks. They looked so—big.

Ignoring the two big Peacemakers, I stood before the woman. Up close, she looked even less like a woman, with a thick neck and wide shoulders. I swallowed hard and asked to see my "husband." I made up a name for him, and thankfully she didn't bother to look him up. She gazed at me for a long moment then said flatly, *No Visitors*.

I then went into my planned tirade, saying I was not taking no for an answer, I had to see my husband, this was an emergency, and if I didn't see him, I would do something drastic. I went on and on about my rights being violated and I was going to get a lawyer until finally the woman signaled the Peacemakers at the doors. I saw them approach and, with a wail of desperation, launched myself over the counter and crashed into the woman.

It was like hitting a brick wall. The woman yelled a curse as I grabbed hold of her shirt, still begging to see my imaginary husband. The two Peacemakers were on me in an instant—one grabbed my leg, nearly wrenching my hip out of its socket. I fought like a wildcat, limbs flailing, screaming at the top of my lungs. I even landed a kick in the Peacemaker's groin before the other one grabbed my arms and wrenched them behind my back. I kept screaming until they put a bag over my head. I felt a sharp jab in my thigh, a heat rushing through my muscles until my vision blurred and faded away.

I awoke in pitch dark. I thought I still had a bag on my head, but then I realized it was just a dark room. I tried to sit up but couldn't—my head felt like a bowling ball. My legs were lead weights.

I was lying on a cot with a small, hard pillow and a thin mattress that smelled like it had been in a damp basement. As my eyes adjusted, I could see the outline of a table, a folding chair, and a narrow window with bars. A door. A small, frayed throw rug. Rain pattered the window—I felt a drop on my face—leaky roof.

After a few minutes, I forced myself to sit up—the room spun and finally settled into place. I figured I must be in one of the camp's cabins, which was not much more than a cell.

There was no lamp, just one overhead light. It took me several more minutes to stand and feel around for a switch, but there wasn't one. I guess the Peacemakers controlled the lights. There was a tiny bathroom with a toilet and shower stall but no curtain. So, this was what the government called "comfortable, hotel-like" accommodations for those forced into quarantine. I tried to remember what Mason had told me—he'd spent months in this place, maybe in a cell just like this one.

I tried the door. Locked. I could open the glass pane of the window a crack. I stripped off a small piece of my red dress and tied it around one of the bars. I left the window open—the rain was soothing.

I talked to You. I prayed for Mason to have done his part and that my diversion worked. That he would get me out of here.

But as the hours ticked by, I got more and more worried. What was taking so long? Something had gone wrong; I was sure of it. I started to get drowsy—maybe the drugs were still in my system, or maybe the adrenaline was making me sleepy. I wondered what time it was—there was no clock in the room. How long was I out? Was it close to morning yet?

I had almost nodded off when I heard the lock click on my door. I sat up, startled. Hopeful. The door opened.

A light shined in my face, so bright I couldn't see who it was. Mason? Is that you?

No answer. He came closer. I shrank back to the wall. It wasn't Mason. Too tall, too broad. A Peacemaker.

What's this? He held up the piece of my dress in the flashlight beam. Did you put that there? Expecting a friend? You know there's no fraternizing allowed here.

Lord, how did he find that tiny piece of cloth? I shook my head and said I didn't know what he was talking about. I'd been dreaming about my husband. That was all.

You're Forbidden, he said. I didn't reply. I thought he would start asking me more questions, why I was there, what I was doing—but he didn't. Instead, he grabbed me by the neck and thrust me down onto the cot. His weight settled on me so I could barely breathe, one knee pressed roughly between my legs, one hand on my neck while the other tugged at my dress. He was…so strong. So heavy. I tried to squirm out from under him, but his hand only tightened on my neck. I kicked up with my knee—he released my neck to hit my face with the back of his hand. Pain shot through me—I saw stars. I went limp, letting my head loll to one side as if he'd knocked me out.

I'm ashamed to say I've had experience with this situation before, in my old life. Maybe no one as big and strong as this Peacemaker, but I knew some tricks. I lay still and let him progress a little in his business until his breath got hot and heavy. Then he seemed to pause, and I peeked one eye open to see him pulling off his face shield and mask. That was it. With my free arm, I reached up and stuck my thumb into his eyeball with all my might. Even a New Person feels that kind of pain. I heard a squishy sound and felt something gush on my thumb—bile rose in the back of my throat, but I didn't let go. He reared back with a loud grunt, and I had a split second to wiggle out of his grasp and scramble for the door, which he had helpfully left unlocked. No one said getting the Cure made you smarter.

An electric jeep sat in front of the cabin—he must have driven up in it. I ran out into the pouring rain, jumped into the driver's seat, and stepped on the pedal just as the Peacemaker burst from the door, growling like some kind of crazed bear. The jeep jerked forward as he launched himself onto the roll bar with a bloodcurdling roar. I shrieked and swerved in crazy circles to shake him off, but he clung like a leech to the side of the jeep. In desperation, I slammed the jeep sidelong into a wall, crushing him—I heard a grunt and felt the whole jeep shudder. I didn't dare look, just jammed the pedal and sped away. The Peacemaker shouted obscenities—I might have hurt him, but in a few seconds, he would be up and chasing me again.

I fought the dizziness, my vision clouding as I struggled to keep the jeep going straight down the road. Where was I going? I had no idea. This was not a part of the plan. I could barely see anything because of the rain. My hands shook so hard that the steering wheel swiveled.

Be strong and courageous. Be strong and courageous.

Suddenly, a light appeared in front of me. A flashlight—another Peacemaker! I didn't stop—I figured I would drive straight into him, run him over if I had to. Surrender was not an option. I was going down fighting.

Stop! Stop! Voices shouted at me. There was more than one. I kept going, gaining speed. I couldn't see much for the rain, just two silhouettes behind the blinding light, waving their arms. They dove out of the way at the last second.

And then I heard my name: Penny!

Gasping, I spun the jeep around and stopped.

Mason?

They ran toward me, pulling off their face masks. It was them, Mason and Blaine. Soaked to the bone, wearing badly fitting Peacemaker uniforms. Get in! I shouted. No time to say more. An alarm sounded—there would soon be more guards after us.

Mason jumped into the driver's seat—I got in the back with Blaine. I glanced at him, his face drawn and thin, his eyes sagging. He looked a hundred years old. But he smiled. I smiled back and hugged him.

Suddenly, there were lights all around us, the whir of drones getting louder. Shouts of alarm, and the guard I'd wounded screaming bloody murder.

What do we do? I asked.

Mason answered by gunning the jeep. Another guard came running out of the shadows to stop us, forcing Mason to swerve so sharply Blaine almost fell out. I snatched him back while gripping the roll bar and stifling a scream. Another jeep came barreling straight toward us—Mason veered onto a narrow walkway between buildings. We were headed straight for the fence.

No, I said. You can't. It's electric. And there are spikes on the top!

Just hang on, Mason said.

We held on, Blaine and I, with a death grip on the roll bar and each other. I prayed out loud: *Be strong and courageous! Do not be afraid! The Lord is with you!*

I expected to feel a jolt of electricity through my body as we crashed through the fence, but it didn't happen. The fence itself broke open as if made of matchsticks rather than steel. I looked back as we drove away to see the other jeep still in pursuit.

Mason drove over a patch of grass and hit a curb, sending Blaine and I nearly airborne. He sped down an empty street and then swerved into a driveway and stopped. We need to run, he said. We could only hope the darkness would shield us from the Peacemakers. What if they had dogs tracking our scent? A thousand what-ifs flooded my mind.

Mason helped Blaine out of the jeep, and we started to run around the back of the house and though an empty parking lot. The sound of our pursuers rang in my ears. As we ran, Mason called Ripley on the walkie. He didn't answer at first—had he been arrested? Were we completely alone? But then Ripley's voice crackled on the walkie—he heard us.

Where are you? He asked. We had no idea. We had arrived at another empty street. I glanced frantically at the few buildings around us. None of them looked familiar. And then I saw a sign on the other side of the street—it was illuminated, glowing, even though there were no lights anywhere else. A church sign, like the kind you can put messages on. It said,

If I be lifted up, I will draw all men unto me.
~ *John 12:32*

Just above the quote were the words, "Glenwood Avenue Church."

Glenwood Avenue! I whisper-shouted into the walkie. There's a church there. Look for the sign! It's lit up!

We ran across the street and hid behind the sign, drenched and shivering. Blaine's breathing sounded more like gasps of pain. We waited to see who would find us first, the Peacemakers or Ripley. It was the longest wait of my life.

Headlights appeared, a car moving slowly toward us. It's Rip! I whispered. I could see the outline of the Mini from the glow of the sign. Mason jumped out and waved him down.

As soon as we were in the car headed for the Hobbit Hole, I started crying. And then I was laughing. And crying again. It was like that all the way home. Laughing and crying, like I didn't know what I was feeling. Like I was feeling everything at the same time.

I know you put that sign there for us.

I didn't find out until later what Mason had done after I'd been arrested. My rant had distracted the Peacemakers in the station enough that he could sneak in and slip through one of those side doors. It was nighttime, so not many Peacemakers were on duty—the place was virtually empty. He found his way to a locker room and stole two uniforms, putting them both on. Then he just walked back out, as if he were one of them. Peacemakers all wear face masks and face shields, so unless you get scanned, no one knows who you are. At least, that's what we were counting on.

He walked around the whole camp for hours, not sure where Blaine was being held. Every building looked the same. But he was able to scope out the camp and check the fence line. He thought if he could steal a jeep, we might be able to drive out the main gate, making some excuse to the guard about moving prisoners. But he didn't see any jeeps.

It was raining hard by then, and Mason was getting worried that the plan was doomed. Then he noticed a Peacemaker standing guard at one of the cabins. Thinking he might get some information, he walked up to the guard and said hello. The guard wasn't very responsive at first, but Mason persisted until the guard started to chat. He revealed that he was guarding "that religious freak" who was being moved the next morning, which the guard was very happy about because the prisoner was always singing, giving the guard a headache. Mason commiserated, then casually offered to take over for him. The guard leaped at the offer, even handing over the key card for the door. Wake him up every hour, the guard instructed. Rough him up if you have to, but don't leave marks. Mason agreed, laughing along with the guard, even though he felt sick.

As soon as the guard was out of sight, Mason used the card and opened the door. Pastor? He said, shining his flashlight into the room. Blaine, lying on a cot, sat up straight and shielded his eyes from the light. He whispered something like Please, leave me alone, not believing at first that it was his friend Mason and not a Peacemaker coming to torture him. I knew how he felt.

After Mason calmed him down, he stripped off the second uniform and told Blaine to put it on. Blaine fumbled with the clothes—he was weak and still shaking. Mason helped him get dressed, and they went out the door, locking it behind them. They went looking for me.

Finding a little piece of cloth tied to a window bar was harder than Mason thought. We'd gotten the idea from Rahab in Jericho—it worked for her, maybe it would work for us, right? Best laid plans. But at night, in the pouring rain, everything looked the same. If it hadn't been for the commotion they heard—my fight with the Peacemaker—they might not have found me at all.

Mason didn't want to tell me ahead of time about his plan to drive through the fence. He knew we would be safe from electric shock as long as we stayed in the vehicle and didn't touch the fence at all. He had half-expected us to take a good portion of the fence with us, but it was a lot flimsier than even he thought. The Ozzies figured the spikes on top and the electrified wires would be enough to scare anyone away from trying to break through, so the hadn't bothered to make the fence itself very strong. Plus, they hadn't counted on Mason.

When I think about what happened, I can't help but be amazed all over again. There's no way we should have gotten away with it. But You. How can I ever thank You enough?

I think that's why I love the psalms. Because they give me the words when I don't have words—when words just aren't enough.

The LORD is close to everyone who calls out to him,
to all who call out to him sincerely.

God shows favor to those who honor him,
listening to their cries for help and saving them.
The LORD protects all who love him,
but he destroys every wicked person.
My mouth will proclaim the LORD's praise,
and every living thing will bless God's holy name forever and always.
~ Psalms 145:18-21

YEAR TWELVE

New Hope

YBR via Shortwave #150

Greetings, Munchkins.

Happy New Year! Remember when we used to say that? Let us never forget that our joy must always be in the Lord and not in this world.

We have much to be thankful for.

Pastor Blaine is safely in the Black Hills, preaching at the church on the reservation. He renamed it New Hope Church. Good name. There were forty natives, along with many of the refugees at his first service, which was more than we expected, though perhaps they came out of curiosity. Let's pray the trend continues, and more people will go not only to hear his amazing escape story but to hear the true gospel and put their faith in Christ.

Let us also be thankful that God has allowed us to continue our work and that our message continues to grow and reach more people all over the world. This is like the days of Acts—for the more persecution we suffer, the more miracles bloom.

There are ten stations that we know of now, some behind enemy lines, for not all Forbidden have moved to the Free States. Keep those who have stayed behind to carry on the work of Christ in your prayers. That would include us here in Kansas.

We have heard from new listeners all over the world—seven stations outside our continent, all of them surviving in the midst of the enemy. We know there are many more who have no radio, no means of communication—those who have gone off the grid completely, hiding out in caves, abandoned warehouses, or underground bunkers. Keep them in your prayers as well.

There is momentous news coming out of New Asgard. Grigori Zazel has made a covenant between the Arabs and Israel, permitting the building of a new temple on the Temple Mount in Jerusalem. They say it will be even grander than the two previous temples and more magnificent than any building ever built. Did we not tell you? Are you listening now?

This is what we in Kansas are saying: take heart. The One who is in you is greater than the one who is in the world. He has overcome the world. All we can do now is be patient and endure. This is our calling.

January 15

Dear God,

I'm coming to the end of my notebook, and I'm not sure I'll be able to find another one. Maybe, on our next trip to SD, I will look. If not, my words and prayers to You will have to stay in my head. I know You will hear them just the same.

On our last trip, we almost got arrested. One of the new Grigori drones intercepted us as we drove through Illinois. Because our car is gas-powered, it couldn't shut us down like it can electric cars, and it didn't have any weapons, but it tried hard to blockade us. If Mason weren't such a crazy driver, challenging the drone to a game of chicken and veering off into a ravine to make it look like we had crashed and burned, we would probably be in a camp now. Or worse. We'll have to lie low and figure out another route to SD. Mason thinks we should get a plane.

I'm just getting tired, I admit. On my dark days, I wonder if this is a battle we can continue to fight. Those are the days that I'm mad at the world for being the world. I know this is all part of The Plan. Thank You for letting me contribute something. I have done something, haven't I? Maybe I'm not Esther, I'm just Penny. But a Penny can still do her part.

I read today what is probably my favorite Psalm of all—it covers all my feelings in just a few short verses. My despair, my longing, my frustration, my anger, my hope, my joy, and my faith.

I can say with confidence that You have, indeed, been good to me.

How long will you forget me, LORD?
Forever?
How long will you hide your face from me?
How long will I be left to my own wits, agony filling my heart?
Daily?

How long will my enemy keep defeating me?
Look at me! Answer me, LORD my God!
Restore sight to my eyes!
Otherwise, I'll sleep the sleep of death,
and my enemy will say, "I won!"
My foes will rejoice over my downfall.
But I have trusted in your faithful love.
My heart will rejoice in your salvation.
Yes, I will sing to the LORD
because he has been good to me.
~ Psalms 13

Acknowledgments

With Appreciation...
To Julie Gwinn, my wonderful agent
To Dawn Carrington, for believing in me
To Kassy Paris, for her helpful editing
To Lisa, for sharing my vision
To the members of Damascus Blades, my intrepid writing group, for all their help in improving this work and keeping me sane
To my husband Steve, for giving me the opportunity to spend my whole day writing
To God, for His grace and for giving me my purpose

Books by Gina Detwiler

About the Author

Gina Detwiler is the author of the YA Supernatural series FOR-LORN and is co-author with Priscilla Shirer of the bestselling middle-grade fantasy series, THE PRINCE WARRIORS. Her non-fiction books include The Ultimate Bible Character Guide and The Ultimate Bible Character Devotional.

She currently lives in Bucks County, Pennsylvania, with her husband, her dog, several imaginary friends, and all of the characters from her books, even the dead ones. She is also the author of three beautiful daughters, for whom she shares credit with her husband, Steve.

Dear Reader

If you enjoyed reading *Penny's Journal*, I would appreciate it if you would help others enjoy this book, too. Here are some of the ways you can help spread the word:

Lend it. This book is lending enabled so please share it with a friend.

Recommend it. Help other readers find this book by recommending it to friends, readers' groups, book clubs, and discussion forums.

Share it. Let other readers know you've read the book by positing a note to your social media account and/or your Goodreads account.

Review it. Please tell others why you liked this book by reviewing it on your favorite ebook site.

Everything you do to help others learn about my book is greatly appreciated!

Gina Detwiler

Plan Your Next Escape!
What's Your Reading Pleasure?

Whether it's captivating historical romance, intriguing mysteries, young adult romance, illustrated children's books, or uplifting love stories, Vinspire Publishing has the adventure for you!

For a complete listing of books available, visit our website at www.vinspirepublishing.com.

Like us on Facebook at
www.facebook.com/VinspirePublishing

Follow us on Twitter at
www.twitter.com/vinspire2004

Follow us on Instagram at
www.instagram.com/vinspirepublishing

and follow our Instagram for details of our upcoming releases, giveaways, author insights, and more!
www.instagram.com/vinspirepublishing

We are your travel guide to your next adventure!

Lightning Source UK Ltd.
Milton Keynes UK
UKHW021304060323
418112UK00022B/971